UNITED IN STRENGTH
BY
LERATO JACKSON MODISE

UNITED IN STRENTGH

First edition. September 24, 2024.

Copyright © 2024 Lerato MODISE.

ISBN: 979-8227264367

Written by Lerato MODISE.

Index

Prologue

Prologue

In the heart of Southern Africa, where mountains rise majestically against the horizon and rivers carve their paths through the land, a story of unity and resilience began to unfold. It was a time when tribes were bound by tradition, yet torn by conflict, and the winds of change whispered through the valleys, carrying with them the dreams of a new era.

At the center of this transformative tale stood King Moshoeshoe I, a leader whose vision transcended the divisions of his time. With a heart attuned to the needs of his people, he sought not just to unify the Basotho, but to forge alliances that would stand against the tides of adversity. Alongside him was the revered prophetess Mantsopa, a woman whose wisdom and spiritual insight guided their journey through the uncertainties of leadership.

Their path was fraught with challenges—hostile tribes, internal dissent, and the weight of history pressing down upon them. Yet, in the face of these trials, they discovered that true strength lay not merely in arms but in the bonds forged through understanding, compassion, and shared purpose.

As the sun set over the mountains, casting a golden hue across the land, the seeds of unity were planted, promising a future where the shadows of doubt could be dispelled by the light of cooperation. This is their story—a chronicle of hope, courage, and the enduring spirit of a people who dared to dream of a world united.

Chapter 1: The Gathering Storm

In the year of storms, when the winds tore across the plains and the rivers swelled with the rains of the highlands, the land of the Basotho was caught in a grip of turmoil. The sky was as restless as the earth, and in that unrest, the kingdom of Moshoeshoe was born—not in glory, but in survival.

Before he was called king, he was known as Lepoqo, son of Mokhachane, chief of the Bamokoteli. From his youth, Lepoqo had shown the qualities of a leader—sharp of mind, patient in council, fierce in battle. But the world into which he was thrust as a young man was a place where such qualities were not enough to guarantee survival.

The great migrations of the time, known as the Difaqane, had torn the region apart. Waves of displaced peoples roamed the land, and the once-peaceful hills were stained with the blood of endless conflicts. Raiders, hungry for land, cattle, and power, descended upon the villages of the southern highlands, leaving ruin in their wake.

It was in these dark days that Lepoqo gathered his people, forging alliances with those scattered and broken by war. Under his leadership, the Basotho grew stronger, yet the threats continued to press in from all sides. From the east came the forces of Shaka Zulu, the spear of their armies reaching as far as the borders of Moshoeshoe's fledgling nation. From the west, the gun-bearing Griqua rode on horseback, raiding with precision. The once fertile land between the Caledon and the Orange River was now a battlefield, and Moshoeshoe knew that to survive, he would need more than warriors—he would need wisdom.

And it was in the midst of this strife that the woman known as Mantsopa came to him.

Her name was whispered among the people, a prophetess whose visions saw beyond the physical world, into the realms of ancestors and spirits. She was said to commune with the land itself, to hear the voices of mountains and rivers. When she arrived at Moshoeshoe's kraal, she carried with her the weight of prophecy.

"Moshoeshoe," she said, for she had already called him by the name he would come to bear—a name that meant 'the shaver,' symbolizing how he shaved away his enemies without shedding unnecessary blood. *"The time has come for you to take your people to higher ground. The land speaks of a place—a mountain surrounded by cliffs, where no enemy may follow. There, you will build a kingdom that no man will tear down."*

Moshoeshoe listened, his eyes narrowing as he considered her words. His mind was sharp, his instinct cautious. He had heard of such prophecies before, and not all had come to pass. Yet, there was something in Mantsopa's presence that stirred him—an ancient force, as if she herself were an embodiment of the earth's will.

"Where is this place?" he asked.

Mantsopa's gaze remained steady. *"It is called Thaba Bosiu, the Mountain of Night. It waits for you, beyond the plains, beyond the reach of those who seek to destroy you. It is a fortress, carved by time and blessed by the spirits."*

The chief's advisors murmured among themselves. Thaba Bosiu was known, but it was a harsh and desolate place, far from the fertile lands they had known. How could they live upon a mountain? How could they sustain themselves in such isolation?

But Moshoeshoe, ever the strategist, saw the truth in her words. In times of great upheaval, survival did not come through abundance, but through security. Thaba Bosiu was impenetrable, its high cliffs offering protection that no valley could provide.

He turned to his father, Mokhachane, who stood by his side. The old chief's face was lined with years of war and wisdom. *"What do you say, Ntate?"*

Mokhachane's eyes flickered to Mantsopa, then back to his son. *"The plains are no longer ours,"* he said quietly. *"The enemies are too many, and the land bleeds with every passing season. If the prophetess speaks truth, then the mountain may be our only hope."*

Moshoeshoe nodded, the decision made in his heart before his lips had even formed the words. "*We will go,*" he said, his voice carrying the authority that only certainty could bring. "*We will climb the mountain, and there we will build a new life.*"

The days that followed were filled with preparation. The people of Moshoeshoe gathered what they could—cattle, grain, tools, and the few possessions that had survived the raids. The journey would be long, and the path would be difficult, but hope had been kindled in their hearts.

On the morning they were to leave, Mantsopa stood before the assembled people, her hands raised to the sky. She spoke in a voice that carried through the air like a song, her words filled with the power of ancient rites.

"*The spirits of the land walk with you,*" she said. "*The ancestors watch over your steps. You will know hardship, but you will also know victory. The mountain will protect you, but you must protect the mountain in return. Take only what is needed, and respect the life it gives.*"

And so they set off, a great migration of the Basotho, led by Moshoeshoe and guided by the unseen hand of prophecy. The sun rose high in the sky as they marched, casting long shadows across the plains. Children clung to their mothers, and warriors walked with their heads held high, their spears glinting in the light.

As the days passed, the land began to change. The flat plains gave way to rolling hills, and the air grew cooler, fresher. The mountain loomed ahead, its dark silhouette rising against the sky like the spine of a sleeping beast. It was a place both inviting and forbidding, a sanctuary and a test.

On the final night before they reached the base of Thaba Bosiu, Moshoeshoe stood apart from his people, gazing up at the mountain. Mantsopa came to him, her presence as quiet as the wind.

"*You have doubts,*" she said, her voice soft but sure.

Moshoeshoe did not turn to face her. "*Doubts are a chief's companion,*" he said. "*I do not fear the mountain, but I wonder if it will be enough. Will the enemy not follow us even here?*"

Mantsopa's gaze remained fixed on the horizon. "*The enemy will come, as they always do. But the mountain will not let them pass. You will build something here that no man can destroy. It has been seen.*"

Moshoeshoe said nothing more, but his heart beat with a new resolve. The prophetess had given him her vision, and now it was up to him to turn that vision into reality.

Chapter 2: The Mountain Beckons

As dawn broke over the horizon, the first light of day illuminated the path ahead, casting a golden glow over the people of Moshoeshoe. They gathered their belongings, the sounds of rustling hides and quiet murmurs filling the air. A sense of purpose had settled among them; today, they would ascend to Thaba Bosiu, the Mountain of Night.

The journey to the mountain was fraught with challenges. The earth beneath their feet was uneven, littered with stones and brush that clawed at their legs. Children were hoisted onto backs, and weary elders leaned on staffs, their faces etched with determination. Yet despite their exhaustion, hope flickered in their eyes—a shared understanding that they were moving toward something greater than themselves.

As they approached the base of the mountain, the air shifted, growing cooler and still. Thaba Bosiu loomed above, its steep cliffs rising like the walls of an ancient fortress. Moshoeshoe halted the procession, allowing his people a moment to take in the sight. He sensed the weight of their collective uncertainty—could this harsh landscape truly become their refuge?

He dismounted and stepped forward, his heart pounding in rhythm with the wind. "*This mountain will be our home,*" he called out, his voice resonating against the stone. "*We will build our lives here, and we will defend it fiercely. Thaba Bosiu is our shield against those who would seek to harm us.*"

The murmurs of doubt quieted, replaced by a growing resolve. Mantsopa stood beside him, her presence a steadying force. She raised her hand, gesturing to the cliffs above. "*The spirits of the mountain await your arrival,*" she declared. "*Climb with respect, and the land will bless you in return.*"

With renewed determination, Moshoeshoe signaled for the ascent to begin. The narrow path wound upward, the rocky terrain challenging their strength and resolve. As they climbed, the sound of their footsteps echoed against the cliffs, a reminder of their struggle and unity.

Each step took them closer to the summit, but the path was treacherous. Loose stones slipped beneath their feet, and the cliffs seemed to loom closer with every upward movement. Moshoeshoe, ever vigilant, moved among his people, offering support to those who faltered and encouragement to those who feared the heights.

At one point, a young boy stumbled, nearly losing his balance on the precarious edge. Moshoeshoe reached out, catching him just in time. The boy looked up at him, eyes wide with fear, and Moshoeshoe knelt beside him, speaking softly. "*Fear not, little one. The mountain will hold you if you trust in its strength.*"

With that, he helped the boy to his feet and continued upward, the boy's small hand clasped tightly in his own. Together, they climbed, each step a testament to their resolve.

As the sun began its descent, painting the sky in hues of orange and pink, they reached the plateau at last—a flat expanse that stretched out like a promise before them. Here, at the top of Thaba Bosiu, the world below seemed to fade away. The land they had fled was now a distant memory, and before them lay the potential for a new beginning.

Moshoeshoe turned to face his people, who emerged onto the plateau, panting but triumphant. "*We stand upon sacred ground,*" he declared, voice strong and clear. "*Here, we will create a kingdom. We will plant our roots deep into this earth, and we will flourish.*"

Mantsopa stepped forward, her eyes sparkling with the light of the setting sun. "*The mountain will provide,*" she said, her voice ringing with certainty. "*But you must give back to it. Care for the land, honor its spirits, and it will protect you.*"

As night fell, the stars emerged in a brilliant display, illuminating the vastness of the sky above. The fires of their camp were lit, and the people gathered around, their spirits lifted by the promise of this new home. Moshoeshoe felt a sense of peace wash over him as he watched his people share stories and laughter, the weight of their burdens momentarily lifted.

Yet, even as he celebrated their arrival, a shadow lingered in his heart. The threats that had chased them from the plains were not far behind, and soon they would need to prepare for the battles that lay ahead. The mountain had given them sanctuary, but it would not shield them from the conflict that defined their world.

The following days were filled with the toil of establishing a community. Moshoeshoe led his people in scouting the plateau, seeking the best locations for water sources and fields for crops. Together, they dug trenches and created small gardens, nurturing the earth with hope and sweat.

Mantsopa walked among them, her presence a calming force. She taught them the old ways of the land—how to recognize the signs of nature, to listen to the whispers of the wind. She spoke of the spirits of their ancestors, urging the people to honor those who had come before them.

As they worked, the mountains seemed to respond to their efforts. Water began to flow from hidden springs, and small patches of green sprouted where they had planted seeds. The Basotho felt a bond forming with the land, an unspoken promise that they would thrive together.

But amid the growth, the specter of conflict loomed. On one fateful night, as Moshoeshoe gazed out over the valley, he spotted a plume of smoke rising in the distance—a signal that their enemies were gathering. He knew the time for peace would be fleeting.

Gathering his warriors, he stood before them as night enveloped the plateau. "We have built our sanctuary, but now we must defend it. The enemies will not relent; they will seek to reclaim what they believe is theirs. We must be prepared."

The warriors nodded, their faces set with determination. They had faced adversity before, and they were ready to stand alongside their chief.

As the stars shone brightly overhead, Moshoeshoe felt a surge of hope. They were not just a people wandering; they were becoming a kingdom, bound by the strength of their unity and the spirit of the land they had chosen to call home.

Chapter 3: The First Skirmish

As the sun rose over Thaba Bosiu, casting golden rays across the plateau, the Basotho awoke to a day filled with purpose. The air was crisp and fresh, infused with the scent of new beginnings. Yet, beneath the tranquility, a tension simmered—a reminder that the peace they sought was fragile, threatened by the encroaching storm of conflict.

Moshoeshoe gathered his warriors at the base of the mountain, the rugged terrain a stark backdrop to their preparations. He stood tall, his presence commanding, the scars of past battles etched on his face serving as a testament to his resilience. His voice rang out, firm and unwavering. *"Today, we prepare for the fight that looms over our home. We must defend Thaba Bosiu, not only for ourselves but for our future generations."*

The warriors, a mix of seasoned fighters and eager youth, nodded in solemn agreement. Among them was Mokhotu, a fierce warrior known for his skill with a spear. His eyes shone with determination, eager to prove himself in the defense of their newfound sanctuary.

As the morning wore on, they conducted drills, sharpening their skills and strategies. The rhythm of clashing weapons echoed across the plateau as they practiced formations, each warrior moving in sync, a living embodiment of unity. Mantsopa watched from a distance, her gaze keen and observant, as if sensing the energy shifting around them.

"Remember," Moshoeshoe called out during their training, *"we fight not just with our strength, but with our minds. The mountain will give us the advantage, but we must remain vigilant."*

The sun climbed higher, illuminating the land below, when a sudden hush fell over the camp. The distant sound of hoof beats echoed in the air, growing louder, a harbinger of the enemy's approach. Moshoeshoe's heart quickened as he turned to face the horizon, where a cloud of dust rose like a dark omen.

"They come!" he shouted, adrenaline surging through his veins. *"To your positions!"*

The warriors sprang into action, taking up their arms, the sounds of metal scraping against leather blending with the pounding of their hearts. They formed a line at the edge of the plateau, their backs against the mountain, the rocky walls a steadfast reminder of the sanctuary they were prepared to defend.

As the riders crested the hill, a fierce sight met their eyes—Mzilikazi, the leader of the Matabele, rode at the front, flanked by his most trusted warriors. His reputation for brutality preceded him, and as his steely gaze swept over the defenders of Thaba Bosiu, Moshoeshoe felt the weight of impending conflict settle heavily in the air.

"Prepare yourselves," he urged his men, his voice steady. *"Hold the line!"*

With a war cry that pierced the stillness, Mzilikazi urged his warriors forward, their horses thundering toward the plateau. Moshoeshoe could feel the ground tremble beneath their charge, a visceral reminder of the fierce battle that was about to unfold.

The clash of steel against steel rang out as the two forces met. The warriors of Moshoeshoe, driven by the fierce resolve to protect their home, stood firm against the onslaught. Spears flashed in the sunlight, and the air filled with shouts and the cries of battle.

Moshoeshoe moved through the fray, his spear a blur as he fought side by side with his men. Each strike was calculated, each movement precise. He felt the weight of responsibility for his people—each warrior fought not just for survival but for the dream of a kingdom that had only just begun to take shape.

As the battle raged, Moshoeshoe caught sight of Mokhotu, skillfully fending off two attackers at once. With a fierce cry, he lunged forward, supporting his fellow warrior. Together, they drove back the enemy, their movements a testament to the bond that had formed among them.

But the Matabele were relentless, and as the fight continued, Moshoeshoe began to sense a shift in the tide. Mzilikazi, his dark figure cutting through the chaos, was now pressing forward, determined to break their line.

With a fierce roar, Moshoeshoe confronted Mzilikazi, the two leaders locking eyes as they approached one another, the clash of their destinies palpable in the air. *"You will not take this land from us!"* Moshoeshoe declared, raising his spear defiantly.

Mzilikazi sneered, his voice a low growl. *"You think a mountain will protect you? You are a fool to think you can stand against my might."*

With that, they clashed, weapons meeting with a resounding force that echoed across the plateau. Moshoeshoe felt the power of the mountain behind him, fueling his resolve as he parried Mzilikazi's blows, searching for an opening.

But the Matabele were skilled warriors, and the fight wore on, both sides pushing against the other with fierce determination. As the sun began to dip toward the horizon, casting long shadows across the battlefield, Moshoeshoe began to sense that victory was within reach.

Drawing upon his training, he feigned a retreat, baiting Mzilikazi into pursuing him. With a sudden shift, Moshoeshoe turned, striking with precision, landing a blow that sent Mzilikazi staggering back. The tide began to turn as the warriors of the Basotho rallied, encouraged by their chief's skill.

With a final rallying cry, Moshoeshoe led his warriors forward, their spirits ignited by the prospect of victory. They surged against the Matabele, pushing them back, reclaiming the ground they had fought so hard to protect.

As dusk settled over the battlefield, the sounds of clashing weapons began to fade, replaced by the weary cheers of victory. The Matabele, realizing their defeat, turned to flee, their once-mighty force scattered like leaves in the wind.

Breathless and bloodied, Moshoeshoe stood among his warriors, surveying the aftermath of the battle. The sun dipped low in the sky, casting a warm glow over the plateau, a stark contrast to the chaos that had just unfolded. His people were safe for now, but the cost of victory weighed heavily on him.

Mantsopa approached, her expression one of calm a midst the storm. *"You have led them well, Moshoeshoe,"* she said, her voice steady. *"But this is only the beginning. The battles to come will be even greater."*

Moshoeshoe nodded, the weight of her words settling in. He understood that the peace they had found atop Thaba Bosiu was fragile, and the enemies that sought to reclaim their land would not rest easily.

As night fell, he gathered his warriors around the fires, tending to the wounded and offering words of gratitude for their bravery. Together, they mourned the losses and celebrated the triumph, their bonds forged in the fires of conflict.

In that moment, as the stars twinkled above, Moshoeshoe felt a sense of purpose take root within him. They had survived the first skirmish, but more challenges lay ahead. Thaba Bosiu was now a symbol of their resilience, and he was determined to transform it into a true kingdom—a place where hope could flourish, and where his people would never again have to fear the dark.

Chapter 4: The Seeds of a Kingdom

In the wake of the battle, the plateau of Thaba Bosiu transformed from a sanctuary of uncertainty into a symbol of resilience. The fires of victory burned brightly in the hearts of the Basotho, but the scars of conflict lingered in the air, a constant reminder that peace was a fleeting treasure.

As dawn broke the following day, Moshoeshoe gathered his people at the foot of the mountain, the rising sun casting long shadows across the ground. The warriors stood proud, their wounds bandaged but their spirits unbroken. Among them, Mokhotu bore a particularly deep cut on his arm, yet he stood tall, determination etched on his face.

"Yesterday, we defended our home," Moshoeshoe began, his voice ringing out like a clarion call. *"But now we must build. We cannot merely survive; we must thrive. Thaba Bosiu will not just be a refuge; it will be a kingdom—a place where our children can grow without fear."*

The crowd murmured in agreement, hope igniting within them. They were weary, yet the fire of purpose surged anew. Mantsopa stepped forward, her presence a beacon of wisdom. *"To build a kingdom, you must first nurture the land. The mountain will yield its gifts, but you must give back. Respect the spirits that dwell here."*

With her guidance, the Basotho set to work, transforming the plateau into a flourishing community. They divided the land, assigning plots for farming and gathering. With each seed planted, they not only cultivated the earth but also their hopes for the future. Moshoeshoe led by example, working alongside his people, his hands calloused by labor but his heart buoyed by their shared vision.

Days turned into weeks, and the once-barren land began to come alive. Green shoots broke through the soil, and the sounds of laughter and song filled the air. Children played among the gardens, while the elders shared stories of their ancestors, weaving the rich tapestry of their culture into the very fabric of their new home.

But as they thrived, the threat of the Matabele remained a specter on the horizon. News of their defeat had spread, but so too had their resolve to reclaim what they believed was rightfully theirs. Moshoeshoe knew that they could not grow complacent; they needed to prepare for the inevitable confrontations that lay ahead.

One evening, as the sun dipped low, Moshoeshoe called for a council with his advisors. They gathered around a large fire, the flickering flames casting dancing shadows on their faces. Mantsopa was present, her expression thoughtful as she listened to the discussions.

"We need to fortify our defenses," Mokhotu suggested, his voice steady. *"If the Matabele return, we must be ready."*

"And we should seek allies," another warrior added. "There are other tribes who share our struggles. If we can unite, we will be stronger."

Moshoeshoe nodded, considering their words. *"Allies are essential, but trust is hard-won in times of war. We must approach with caution."*

Mantsopa interjected, her voice calm but firm. *"Listen to the land, for it will guide you. There are those who respect the spirits and those who do not. Seek out the ones who understand the balance of nature and the importance of community."*

Moshoeshoe's mind raced with possibilities. He knew that the tribes of the region were as diverse as the landscapes that surrounded them, each with its own customs and traditions. Some were allies, while others had histories of conflict. Finding the right balance would be key to forging lasting alliances.

"Tomorrow," he said, determination shining in his eyes, *"I will travel to the nearby clans. I will extend our hand in friendship, but I will also show them the strength we possess."*

The council nodded, a sense of purpose settling over them. They would stand together, united not only in their struggle but in their vision for the future.

As the fire crackled, the warriors shared stories of bravery and hope, laughter mingling with the smoke. Moshoeshoe felt the weight of responsibility upon him but also the warmth of camaraderie, a reminder that he was not alone in this endeavor.

The following day, as the sun rose in the east, Moshoeshoe set out on his journey, accompanied by Mokhotu and a small band of trusted warriors. The path wound down the mountain, the familiar terrain now transformed by their growing sense of purpose. The air was alive with the sounds of nature, a gentle reminder of the land they fought to protect.

Their first stop was the village of the Tlokwa, known for their skilled craftsmen and rich culture. As they approached, Moshoeshoe could see the vibrant colors of their woven baskets and hear the rhythmic beats of drums in the distance. He felt a mixture of hope and trepidation—would they welcome him as a friend or view him as a threat?

As they entered the village, the atmosphere shifted. The Tlokwa warriors eyed them warily, suspicion etched on their faces. Moshoeshoe stepped forward, his heart pounding but his resolve unyielding.

"*I am Moshoeshoe of the Basotho,*" he announced, his voice clear and strong. "*I come not as an enemy, but as a friend. Together, we can stand against those who threaten our lands and our people.*"

The chief of the Tlokwa, a stout man with a long beard and piercing eyes, stepped forward. "*We have heard tales of your courage, Moshoeshoe,*" he said cautiously. "*But many have come to us with promises. What guarantees do we have that you will not turn on us?*"

Moshoeshoe met the chief's gaze, unwavering. "*Our survival depends on unity. I offer not just words but an alliance forged in trust. Together, we can create a force that protects our lands and our families.*"

After a tense silence, the chief nodded slowly. "*Very well. We shall hear what you have to say, but know that trust is earned, not given. Prove your intentions, and you may find a true ally in the Tlokwa.*"

As the day wore on, Moshoeshoe shared stories of their struggles, the victories won and the hardships endured. The warmth of the fire flickered between them, illuminating the path toward understanding. In time, the walls of suspicion began to crumble, replaced by a growing sense of camaraderie.

As evening fell, the Tlokwa chief extended an invitation for Moshoeshoe and his warriors to stay for the night, a gesture of goodwill that sparked a glimmer of hope in Moshoeshoe's heart. Together, they feasted on roasted meat and shared laughter, their spirits lifting in unison.

But as night enveloped the village, Moshoeshoe could not shake the feeling that shadows lingered just beyond the light. The Matabele would not be deterred, and with each passing moment, he knew they were still plotting their next move.

The following days were filled with similar visits, forging connections with neighboring tribes—the Batlokoa, the Bakone, and others. With each gathering, Moshoeshoe extended his hand in friendship, emphasizing the strength that unity could bring. Slowly but surely, the seeds of a coalition began to take root.

As the sun dipped low in the sky one evening, casting a warm glow over the gathering of allied leaders at Thaba Bosiu, Moshoeshoe stood before them. The warriors, chiefs, and elders from various tribes surrounded him, their faces filled with determination and hope.

"*This is the beginning,*" Moshoeshoe declared, his voice rising with fervor. "*Together, we will protect our homes and our people. We are not just defending a mountain; we are building a kingdom—a place where our children will know peace and prosperity.*"

The crowd erupted in applause, their spirits soaring as they joined in a shared vision. In that moment, Moshoeshoe felt the weight of the future resting upon him, but he was no longer alone. Together, they would face whatever challenges lay ahead, united in purpose and resolve.

As the night deepened and the stars illuminated the sky, Moshoeshoe looked around at the faces of his allies—faces that now held the promise of a future brighter than any of them had dared to dream.

Chapter 5: Shadows of War

The newfound alliance among the Basotho and their neighboring tribes breathed life into the plateau of Thaba Bosiu. Plans were set in motion, strategies discussed, and training intensified. Moshoeshoe felt a surge of hope; they were no longer merely survivors—they were a united force.

Yet, even as preparations unfolded, the specter of the Matabele loomed larger. News from scouts reported increased activity among Mzilikazi's forces, their camps growing in number and boldness. Moshoeshoe knew that their enemies were regrouping, plotting their next move.

One evening, as the sun sank low, painting the sky in shades of crimson and gold, Moshoeshoe gathered his warriors at the base of Thaba Bosiu. The air buzzed with a mixture of excitement and anxiety, the gravity of the situation palpable.

"We stand at a precipice," Moshoeshoe began, his voice steady. *"The Matabele are not far from us. We have built alliances, but we must prepare for the battles that lie ahead. It is not just our lives that hang in the balance; it is the future of our people."*

Mokhotu stepped forward, his expression fierce. *"We must strike first. Show them that we will not cower in the shadows of fear."*

A murmur of agreement rippled through the group, but Mantsopa raised her hand, silencing the room. *"We must not act out of desperation. A hasty strike could cost us dearly. We need to gather intelligence and understand their movements before making any decisions."*

Moshoeshoe nodded, acknowledging her wisdom. *"You are right, Mantsopa. We will send scouts to assess their numbers and their strategies. We must be calculated in our response."*

The following days were filled with tension as the warriors prepared for the inevitable clash. Scouts were dispatched under the cover of darkness, slipping into the terrain to gather vital information. The anticipation hung thick in the air, a taut string waiting to snap.

One evening, as Moshoeshoe and his council convened, a scout burst into the meeting, breathless and covered in dust. *"They gather in numbers, Chief! Mzilikazi has united several clans. They plan to attack within days!"*

The room fell silent, the gravity of the news settling over them like a heavy cloak. Moshoeshoe's heart raced. They had little time to fortify their defenses and prepare for battle.

"We must send word to our allies," he said, steeling himself. *"They need to know that the time for action is upon us."*

The council worked quickly, sending messengers to the various tribes, urging them to join their cause. As the sun set, casting long shadows across the land, warriors began to assemble, their spirits ignited by the urgency of their mission.

Training intensified, each warrior honing their skills, sharpening their weapons, and preparing their minds for the conflict that lay ahead. Moshoeshoe moved among them, offering words of encouragement, instilling a sense of unity and purpose. They were more than individual fighters; they were a collective force, a rising tide against the threat of destruction.

The night before the anticipated attack, Moshoeshoe stood atop Thaba Bosiu, gazing out over the land. The stars twinkled above, a reminder of the ancestors who had fought for their people before him. He felt their presence, a guiding light in the darkness.

As he descended the mountain, he found Mantsopa sitting by a fire, her expression contemplative. *"You carry a heavy burden,"* she said softly, her voice like a whisper in the night.

"I feel the weight of our future," Moshoeshoe admitted. *"If we fail, all we have built will crumble. I fear for our people."*

Mantsopa nodded, her gaze steady. *"But you are not alone. The strength of your people will carry you through. Trust in them, and trust in the land. It has seen many battles, and it will see many more."*

As dawn broke, the atmosphere shifted, charged with anticipation. The allied forces gathered at the foot of Thaba Bosiu, their banners flying high, a kaleidoscope of colors representing the unity they had forged. Moshoeshoe stood at the forefront, surveying the gathered warriors, their faces a blend of determination and fear.

"We fight not just for ourselves," he proclaimed, his voice echoing across the ranks. *"We fight for our families, our future, and our land. Together, we will show the Matabele that we are strong and unyielding!"*

With a unified roar, the warriors raised their weapons in the air, the sound reverberating through the valley. It was a moment of solidarity, a promise of unwavering support a midst the storm that was about to unfold.

As they moved toward the battlefield, the sun rose higher, illuminating their path. The terrain was familiar, yet each step felt like a march toward destiny. Moshoeshoe led the way, his heart steady despite the turmoil within.

They reached the field where the Matabele had gathered, their numbers vast and imposing. Mzilikazi stood at the forefront, a figure of authority and menace, his warriors arrayed behind him, ready for battle.

Moshoeshoe raised his spear, signaling his forces to halt. *"Let us not begin with bloodshed! We offer you a chance for peace, Mzilikazi! Join us as allies, not enemies!"*

Mzilikazi's laughter echoed across the field, a sound devoid of warmth. *"You think you can sway me with words? You are a fool to think I would ally with those I intend to conquer!"*

With a wave of his hand, the Matabele surged forward, their battle cries ringing out in defiance. Moshoeshoe steeled himself, his heart pounding as the two forces clashed, the air thick with the sounds of battle.

As the fight unfolded, chaos erupted around him. Warriors fell, and the ground soaked in the blood of both sides. Moshoeshoe fought fiercely, his spear striking true as he moved through the fray, determined to protect his people.

Mokhotu fought by his side, a fierce warrior a midst the chaos. *"We must break their lines!"* he shouted, his voice cutting through the din. *"If we can reach Mzilikazi, we can turn the tide!"*

With a fierce nod, Moshoeshoe pressed forward, cutting a path through the tumult. They fought with every ounce of strength, their bodies moving in harmony, driven by the bond they had forged in the fires of preparation.

But as they approached Mzilikazi, a sudden onslaught from the Matabele pushed them back. Moshoeshoe felt a surge of frustration, a tightening of desperation as he struggled against the tide.

Just then, a figure caught his eye—Mantsopa, standing at the edge of the battlefield, her hands raised in an ancient gesture. The winds shifted around her, and he felt the energy of the land responding to her call.

"Trust the land!" she shouted, her voice rising above the chaos. *"It will guide you!"*

Drawing upon the strength of the mountain, Moshoeshoe rallied his warriors. *"For our people! For Thaba Bosiu!"* he roared, igniting the fire of determination within them.

Together, they surged forward once more, united in purpose. With each strike, each cry of defiance, they pushed against the Matabele, their resolve hardening like iron.

As the battle raged on, Moshoeshoe and Mokhotu reached Mzilikazi. The two leaders faced one another, their eyes locked in a fierce contest of wills. *"You will not take our home,"* Moshoeshoe declared, his voice resolute.

With a powerful clash of weapons, they engaged in a brutal duel, the sounds of their struggle drowned out by the chaos around them. Each strike reverberated with the weight of their peoples' hopes and dreams.

But as fatigue set in, Moshoeshoe could feel the tide beginning to turn. Drawing upon the energy of the land, he summoned every ounce of strength left within him. With a final, desperate thrust, he aimed for Mzilikazi's heart.

The blow landed true, sending the Matabele leader staggering back, shock and fury etched on his face. With their chief wounded, the Matabele forces began to falter, uncertainty rippling through their ranks.

The Basotho seized the moment, rallying together, their spirits ignited by the sight of their leader's victory. They surged forward, driving the Matabele back, reclaiming the ground they had fought so hard to protect.

As the sun dipped below the horizon, casting the battlefield in hues of gold and crimson, the sounds of conflict began to fade. The Matabele, now in disarray, turned and fled, their spirits shattered by the loss of their leader.

Breathless and bloodied, Moshoeshoe stood among his warriors, the weight of victory settling heavily upon him. They had defended their home, but at what cost? He looked around at his people, a mixture of relief and grief etched on their faces.

Mantsopa approached, her expression solemn yet proud. *"You have led them well, Moshoeshoe. The spirits of the land have smiled upon you today."*

As they gathered together, mourning their losses and celebrating their triumphs, Moshoeshoe felt a profound sense of purpose solidifying within him. They had not only defended their sanctuary; they had forged a kingdom in the heart of the storm.

In the aftermath of battle, as the stars twinkled above, he realized that their struggle was far from over. But united, they would face whatever challenges lay ahead, ready to cultivate the seeds of a kingdom that would stand the test of time.

Chapter 6: The Aftermath of War

As the first light of dawn crept over the horizon, the battlefield bore silent witness to the night's brutal struggle. The air was thick with the scent of earth and sweat, mingled with the remnants of smoke from the fires that had burned through the night. Moshoeshoe surveyed the scene, his heart heavy with the weight of both victory and loss.

His warriors were weary but triumphant, their spirits lifted by the sight of their enemies in retreat. Yet, amid the celebrations, the toll of the battle hung heavily in the air. He could see the faces of those who had fought valiantly, many marred by grief and fatigue. The losses were palpable, and he felt a sense of responsibility to honor them.

"Gather around!" he called, his voice steady but soft. The warriors formed a circle, and Moshoeshoe looked into the eyes of each one, their faces illuminated by the rising sun. *"Today, we honor those who fought and fell. They were brave souls who stood for our people, our land. Let us remember them not with sorrow, but with gratitude for their sacrifice."*

The crowd nodded, a solemn agreement echoing in their hearts. They bowed their heads as Moshoeshoe offered a prayer to the ancestors, invoking their spirits to guide the fallen to peace. The warriors joined in, their voices blending in a harmonious chant that reverberated through the valley, a tribute to the strength of their unity.

Once the ceremony concluded, the mood shifted from mourning to resolve. *"We have pushed back the Matabele, but they will regroup,"* Moshoeshoe warned, his gaze fierce. *"We must prepare ourselves for what is to come. The path to peace is fraught with challenges, but together, we are stronger."*

Mokhotu stepped forward, a fierce glint in his eye. *"We should fortify our defenses and send scouts to watch for any sign of Mzilikazi's return. We cannot allow our guard to drop."*

The council agreed, and the next few days were consumed with preparation. They strengthened their positions around Thaba Bosiu, reinforcing the walls with stones and logs, and training tirelessly to hone their skills. Moshoeshoe ensured that every warrior, young and old, was prepared to defend their home.

A midst this flurry of activity, Mantsopa was busy in her own way, drawing upon the wisdom of the land. She spent her days in the fields, gathering herbs and speaking to the spirits of the ancestors, seeking guidance for the trials ahead. Her connection to the land was a source of strength for the warriors, a reminder of their roots.

As the days turned into weeks, Moshoeshoe held meetings with his allied tribes, ensuring that they remained united in purpose. They shared resources, stories, and strategies, weaving their fates together into a fabric of resilience.

One evening, as the sun dipped below the horizon, Moshoeshoe gathered the leaders of the allied tribes at Thaba Bosiu. The air crackled with anticipation as they took their places around the fire, the flames casting flickering shadows on their faces.

"I stand before you today, not just as your chief, but as a brother in arms," Moshoeshoe began. *"We have faced our first test together and emerged stronger. But we cannot afford to be complacent. Mzilikazi will not forget this defeat, and we must be prepared for the next confrontation."*

The murmurs of agreement rippled through the gathering, each leader understanding the gravity of the situation. The chief of the Tlokwa, his voice steady, spoke up. *"We are with you, Moshoeshoe. Our people have suffered too, and we will not stand idly by while the Matabele threaten our existence."*

A sense of camaraderie filled the air, and Moshocshoe felt a surge of hope. They were no longer merely a collection of tribes; they were forging a kingdom together, bound by shared struggles and a common vision.

As the meeting progressed, Mantsopa shared insights she had gleaned from her connection to the land. *"The spirits tell me that we must not only prepare for war but also nurture the bonds we have forged. We should establish trade and cultural exchanges to strengthen our unity."*

The leaders nodded, recognizing the wisdom in her words. Moshoeshoe felt a renewed sense of purpose, understanding that their survival depended not only on strength but also on the relationships they nurtured.

In the weeks that followed, the allied tribes worked together, establishing trade routes and cultural exchanges. They shared agricultural techniques, taught each other songs and dances, and strengthened their ties in ways that transcended the mere alliances formed out of necessity.

However, the shadow of the Matabele still loomed over them. Scouts reported that Mzilikazi was rallying more warriors, seeking vengeance for his defeat. The urgency of their preparations intensified, and Moshoeshoe felt the weight of impending conflict pressing down on his shoulders.

One evening, as the sun set in a blaze of orange and pink, Moshoeshoe stood at the edge of Thaba Bosiu, gazing out over the land. The beauty of the landscape filled him with a sense of calm, yet the foreboding tension lingered in the air.

Mantsopa approached, her presence soothing. *"You worry for your people,"* she said softly. *"But you must remember that strength lies not only in the sword but in the heart of the people. They trust you."*

"I fear what lies ahead," Moshoeshoe admitted, his voice tinged with vulnerability. *"Every decision I make carries the weight of their lives. I want to protect them, but what if I lead them into darkness?"*

Mantsopa placed a reassuring hand on his shoulder. *"Trust in the land and in your people. You are their leader for a reason. Listen to their voices, for they are the heartbeat of this kingdom."*

Inspired by her words, Moshoeshoe took a deep breath, grounding himself in the moment. He understood that leadership was a shared burden, one he would carry with the support of his people and the wisdom of the land.

The days turned into weeks as the alliance solidified, yet the Matabele remained a constant threat. Mzilikazi's forces were growing, and Moshoeshoe knew that the time for confrontation was approaching.

One fateful morning, as the sun rose over Thaba Bosiu, word arrived that Mzilikazi was marching toward them with an army twice the size of theirs. The time for preparation was over; the moment for action had come.

Gathering his warriors and allies, Moshoeshoe prepared for the final battle. *"This is our moment,"* he declared, his voice echoing across the assembled forces. *"We fight not just for our survival but for our future. Together, we will show Mzilikazi that the spirit of the Basotho and our allies is unbreakable!"*

With that rallying cry, they set out toward the battlefield, hearts beating in unison, ready to face whatever challenges lay ahead. The mountain stood tall behind them, a testament to their resilience, as they marched into the unknown.

Chapter 7: The Final Stand

The sun hung low in the sky as Moshoeshoe and his assembled forces approached the battlefield. The air was thick with tension, the weight of anticipation pressing down on them like a heavy cloak. Each warrior carried a fire in their heart, fueled by the knowledge that their very existence depended on this fight.

As they reached the edge of the valley, Moshoeshoe halted the procession, turning to face his people. The sight before him was both awe-inspiring and daunting. Warriors from the Basotho and allied tribes stood shoulder to shoulder, their faces a tapestry of determination, fear, and unwavering resolve.

"Mzilikazi believes he can crush us," Moshoeshoe began, his voice resonating with authority. *"But he underestimates our strength, our unity. Today, we stand not as individuals, but as one. We are the guardians of our land, and we will fight to the last breath to protect what is ours!"*

A powerful roar erupted from the crowd, their battle cries echoing through the valley. The sound reverberated in Moshoeshoe's chest, igniting a fierce pride within him. They were ready.

As the opposing forces of the Matabele came into view, Moshoeshoe felt a chill run down his spine. Mzilikazi stood at the forefront, a fearsome sight clad in feathers and animal hides, his warriors arrayed behind him like a dark storm cloud. The Matabele marched with a confidence that came from their reputation, but they had yet to face the united spirit of the Basotho.

With a swift signal, Moshoeshoe led his warriors forward, the ground trembling beneath their feet. The tension in the air crackled as the two armies met in a clash that shook the very earth. The sounds of metal striking metal, the cries of warriors, and the war drums resonated in a cacophony of chaos.

Mokhotu fought valiantly at Moshoeshoe's side, cutting through the ranks of the Matabele. *"We must break their lines!"* he shouted, urging the warriors forward. The Basotho surged ahead, determined to turn the tide of battle.

Moshoeshoe fought with every ounce of strength, his spear dancing through the air, striking true against his foes. Yet, amidst the chaos, he was acutely aware of the price of war—the faces of those he fought beside, the echoes of their laughter now replaced by the grim reality of conflict.

As the battle raged on, Moshoeshoe spotted Mzilikazi in the distance, his formidable presence commanding the Matabele forces. He felt a surge of determination—he needed to confront the Matabele leader directly to rally his people and sow doubt among the enemy.

With a fierce battle cry, Moshoeshoe fought his way through the chaos, pushing forward with Mokhotu at his side. As they approached Mzilikazi, the Matabele leader met their charge head-on, his warriors parting like a wave to reveal their chief.

"Moshoeshoe!" Mzilikazi bellowed, his voice cutting through the din of battle. *"You are a fool to come here! You will only meet your end!"*

"I will not cower before you, Mzilikazi!" Moshoeshoe shouted back, raising his spear high. *"Today, we fight not just for our survival but for the legacy of our people!"*

With that, the two leaders clashed, their weapons colliding with a force that sent shock waves through the battlefield. Moshoeshoe focused on Mzilikazi's every move, determined to outmancuver the seasoned warrior. They exchanged blows, each strike resonating with the weight of their respective peoples' hopes.

As the battle raged around them, the tide began to turn. The unity of the Basotho and their allies shone through, their spirit unwavering against the fierce onslaught of the Matabele. Moshoeshoe could feel the energy of the land flowing through him, a reminder of the strength that lay beneath their feet.

Just as Moshoeshoe gained the upper hand, he felt a sudden pain rip through his side. He glanced down to see a Matabele warrior, hidden among the chaos, had struck him. Blood seeped through his fingers as he staggered, but determination surged within him.

"*Mokhotu!*" he called, his voice strained but resolute.

Mokhotu surged forward, dispatching the attacker with a swift blow. "*Stay strong, Chief! We need you!*"

With renewed vigor, Moshoeshoe pushed through the pain, the sight of his warriors rallying around him igniting a fire within. He would not falter; he would lead them to victory.

With one final push, Moshoeshoe and Mokhotu broke through the Matabele lines, drawing closer to Mzilikazi. Their duel intensified, each man's strength tested to its limits. Moshoeshoe could feel the weight of his people's hopes resting on his shoulders, and he drew upon every ounce of resolve he possessed.

With a decisive strike, he aimed for Mzilikazi's heart, and as their weapons collided one last time, he channeled the spirit of his ancestors, the strength of the land, and the unity of his people. The impact sent Mzilikazi staggering back, shock etched across his face.

The Matabele forces, witnessing their leader's falter, began to waver. The morale of the Basotho surged, and the roar of triumph echoed across the battlefield. Mzilikazi, now vulnerable, looked to his warriors, but doubt had crept into their hearts.

Seizing the moment, Moshoeshoe raised his spear high. "*This is our land! Our people! We will not be defeated!*" His voice rang out, igniting the spirits of those around him.

With that rallying cry, the Basotho surged forward, overwhelming the Matabele forces. The tide had turned, and the warriors fought with renewed strength, pushing their enemies back.

As the sun began to set, casting a golden light over the battlefield, Moshoeshoe felt the weight of victory in the air. The Matabele, now in disarray, retreated, their once-mighty forces crumbling before the unity and determination of the Basotho and their allies.

In the aftermath of the battle, as the dust settled and the cries of victory rang out, Moshoeshoe sank to his knees, the exhaustion washing over him. He felt the pain of his wounds but also the overwhelming relief of having defended his people.

Mokhotu knelt beside him, a triumphant grin on his face. "*We did it, Chief! We stood together, and we prevailed!*"

As the sun dipped below the horizon, painting the sky with hues of orange and purple, Moshoeshoe looked around at the faces of his people—bruised, bloodied, but unbroken. They had fought fiercely and unitedly, their spirit undeniable.

"*Today, we have shown the world that we are strong, that we will not be defeated,*" Moshoeshoe proclaimed, his voice filled with conviction. "*This is not just a victory for us, but for all those who seek peace and unity. We will rebuild, and together, we will thrive.*"

The warriors erupted in cheers, their voices rising to the heavens, a testament to their resilience. The battle may have been won, but the journey to cultivate their kingdom had just begun.

As night fell over Thaba Bosiu, Moshoeshoe felt the presence of his ancestors surrounding him, their spirits guiding him forward. They had faced darkness and emerged into the light, ready to forge a future that honored their sacrifices.

Together, they would build a kingdom worthy of their dreams.

Chapter 8: A New Dawn

The aftermath of the battle was a time of reflection and rebuilding. As the first light of dawn broke over the horizon, Moshoeshoe stood atop Thaba Bosiu, surveying the land that now belonged to the united tribes of the Basotho. The once-bloodied ground was beginning to heal, the vibrant hues of dawn painting a picture of hope.

The warriors were busy gathering the remnants of the battlefield, honoring their fallen comrades with solemn rites. Moshoeshoe felt a profound sense of responsibility. They had emerged victorious, but the cost weighed heavily on his heart. The faces of those who had fought bravely were imprinted in his mind, their sacrifices a reminder of the fragility of life.

As he descended the mountain, Moshoeshoe was met by Mantsopa, her expression one of quiet strength. *"The spirits of our ancestors are with us, Moshoeshoe. They have witnessed our struggles and our triumphs. We must honor them by nurturing the bonds we have forged."*

"I know," he replied, his voice tinged with sorrow. *"But the loss of our brothers and sisters is still fresh. I fear that as we move forward, we might forget the weight of their sacrifice."*

Mantsopa placed a reassuring hand on his shoulder. *"We honor them by living fully, by ensuring their sacrifices were not in vain. Let their memory inspire us to build a better future."*

With her words echoing in his heart, Moshoeshoe set about the task of rebuilding. The next few weeks were filled with activity as the allied tribes came together to mend what had been broken. They cleared the battlefield, burying their fallen with dignity and respect, erecting markers that honored their bravery.

The bonds between the tribes deepened as they worked side by side, sharing stories and laughter, the pain of the past transforming into a shared resolve for the future. Moshoeshoe understood that this was more than just reconstruction; it was the foundation of a new nation, one built on unity and resilience.

In the evenings, they gathered around the fire, sharing songs and tales of their ancestors. Mantsopa led the gatherings, her connection to the spiritual world guiding them as she spoke of the importance of community and harmony with the land.

"We are the keepers of this earth," she reminded them. *"Our strength lies in our ability to listen to its whispers and to care for one another. We must cultivate not only our fields but our hearts."*

As the seasons changed, the Basotho found strength in their collective identity. Trade routes were established, and the tribes exchanged goods, ideas, and cultural practices. The unity forged in battle blossomed into a vibrant community, rich in diversity and shared purpose.

However, as peace settled over Thaba Bosiu, the specter of Mzilikazi still lingered in the minds of the people. They knew that he would not easily forget his defeat. Moshoeshoe felt a weight of urgency to ensure that their newfound alliance remained steadfast against any future threats.

One evening, Moshoeshoe called a council meeting with the leaders of the allied tribes. They gathered around a large fire, the flames flickering against the darkening sky. *"We have built much since our victory,"* he began, looking around at the faces of his allies. *"But we cannot rest easy. Mzilikazi will not abandon his ambitions. We must be prepared for what lies ahead."*

The chief of the Tlokwa nodded in agreement. *"We should fortify our defenses and keep scouts on alert. We cannot afford to be caught off guard again."*

Mantsopa spoke up, her voice steady. *"While we prepare for conflict, we must also continue to foster our relationships. Strengthening our bonds will be our greatest defense against those who seek to divide us."*

Moshoeshoe considered her words, recognizing the wisdom in her perspective. *"You are right. We will build not only walls to protect us but also ties that will hold us together. Let us focus on nurturing our community and preparing for any challenges that may arise."*

The council agreed, and they set about creating a plan. They would train their warriors while also establishing community projects—agricultural initiatives, educational gatherings, and cultural festivals that celebrated their unity.

As the months passed, the Basotho flourished. Crops grew abundantly, and trade flourished, bringing prosperity to their lands. Moshoeshoe took pride in witnessing the fruits of their labor, the vibrant community thriving under the shared vision of peace.

But one fateful day, scouts returned with alarming news. Mzilikazi was gathering forces once more, his ambitions reignited by the desire for revenge. The tension that had been building now became a tangible threat.

Moshoeshoe called an emergency council meeting, the gravity of the situation palpable in the air. *"We have seen what Mzilikazi is capable of,"* he said, his voice steady despite the turmoil within. *"We must prepare our people for another battle. This time, we fight not only for survival but for the future we have built together."*

The warriors steeled themselves, their determination unwavering. As preparations began, Moshoeshoe felt the weight of history upon him. He understood that this confrontation would not only determine their fate but also shape the legacy they would leave for generations to come.

With Mantsopa by his side, he reminded his people of the strength they had shown in their previous struggle. *"We are more than warriors; we are a community, a family. Together, we will face whatever comes our way. We will not be broken!"*

As the sun set over Thaba Bosiu, casting long shadows across the land, Moshoeshoe felt a surge of resolve. They had overcome so much, and this time, they would stand united against the storm that approached.

Chapter 9: The Gathering Storm

The days leading up to the impending conflict were filled with a sense of urgency. As the sun rose each morning, casting a warm glow over Thaba Bosiu, Moshoeshoe felt the weight of anticipation pressing down on his shoulders. His warriors trained tirelessly, their spirits unyielding, but the specter of Mzilikazi loomed larger with each passing moment.

Moshoeshoe gathered his council once more, the air thick with determination. *"We must anticipate Mzilikazi's moves,"* he urged, his voice steady. *"He is a cunning strategist, and we cannot afford to underestimate him. We will not only prepare for battle but also seek to understand our enemy's motivations."*

Mantsopa nodded, her expression thoughtful. *"It is crucial that we know not just the enemy's strength but also their weaknesses. We must remember that they, too, are driven by fear and desire. If we can find a way to exploit that, we might gain the upper hand without bloodshed."*

The council members murmured in agreement, recognizing the wisdom in her words. Moshoeshoe felt a spark of hope. Perhaps there was a way to confront Mzilikazi that didn't solely rely on conflict.

They spent the following days strategizing, sending scouts to gather intelligence on the Matabele forces. As the reports trickled in, Moshoeshoe and his allies began to piece together Mzilikazi's plans. The Matabele were indeed rallying strength, but they were also facing challenges—discontent among their ranks and shortages of resources.

"His warriors may be fierce," Moshoeshoe remarked during a strategy session, *"but they are not invincible. If we can create divisions within his ranks, we may force them to reconsider their path."*

With this new approach in mind, the council devised a plan. They would reach out to the tribes that had once aligned with Mzilikazi, seeking to sow seeds of doubt and encourage defection. Mantsopa agreed to lead a group of emissaries, using her wisdom and connection to the spirits to negotiate peace where possible.

As Mantsopa prepared for her journey, Moshoeshoe felt a mix of pride and concern. *"Be careful,"* he urged, placing a hand on her shoulder. *"You carry the hopes of our people with you. Your strength lies not just in words but in the spirit you embody."*

She smiled gently, her confidence radiating. *"I will speak from the heart, Moshoeshoe. We fight not just for ourselves but for a future that embraces all tribes, including those who have lost their way."*

With a small entourage, Mantsopa set out, journeying through the valleys and hills to seek those willing to listen. Meanwhile, Moshoeshoe intensified training for his warriors, ensuring they remained ready for any confrontation.

As days turned into weeks, the tension in the air grew palpable. The winds of change blew through the land, stirring anticipation and anxiety among the people. News of Mantsopa's mission began to filter back, and a mixture of hope and uncertainty filled the hearts of the Basotho.

One evening, as Moshoeshoe stood on the edge of Thaba Bosiu, gazing out at the horizon, he was joined by Mokhotu. *"Do you think she will succeed?"* Mokhotu asked, concern etched across his face.

"She possesses a strength we cannot see," Moshoeshoe replied, his gaze unwavering. *"She speaks the language of the land and the hearts of the people. If anyone can reach them, it is Mantsopa."*

Their conversation was interrupted by the arrival of a scout, breathless and urgent. *"Chief! Mantsopa has returned!"*

A wave of relief washed over Moshoeshoe as he hurried to the gathering place. Mantsopa stood there, her presence commanding even a midst the weariness of travel. The council gathered around her, eager to hear her news.

"I have spoken with several tribes," she began, her voice steady. *"Many are discontent with Mzilikazi's leadership. They are weary of endless conflict and are seeking a path toward peace. However, they need assurance that we can protect them."*

Moshoeshoe felt hope bloom within him. *"What do we need to do?"* he asked, focused on the possibilities.

"We must extend our hand," Mantsopa replied, her eyes shining with resolve. *"Offer them a place among us, a chance to unite for a common purpose. If they see that we stand strong together, they will be more willing to join our cause."*

The council discussed the proposal, recognizing the wisdom in Mantsopa's approach. They would send messengers to the tribes, inviting them to a gathering at Thaba Bosiu to discuss the future of their lands. It would be a bold move, but one that could shift the balance of power.

As the invitations were sent, Moshoeshoe felt a sense of trepidation mixed with hope. He knew that Mzilikazi would not stand idly by while they sought to build alliances. The gathering at Thaba Bosiu would be crucial not only for their future but also for the legacy they would leave behind.

Days passed, and one by one, representatives from the neighboring tribes began to arrive at Thaba Bosiu. The atmosphere was thick with anticipation as they gathered around the fire, the flames flickering in the twilight.

Moshoeshoe addressed the crowd, his voice ringing out over the assembled leaders. *"We stand here not as separate tribes but as a community bound by a shared vision. We have faced adversity and emerged stronger, but our future depends on our unity. Together, we can create a land where peace reigns, where our children can grow without the shadow of war."*

The representatives listened, some nodding in agreement, while others exchanged skeptical glances. Mantsopa stepped forward, her presence magnetic. *"This is an opportunity for all of us. We can break the cycle of conflict and work toward a future that honors our ancestors and embraces the generations to come."*

As the discussions unfolded, the air was charged with both hope and uncertainty. Some tribes expressed willingness to join, while others hesitated, wary of Mzilikazi's retribution. Moshoeshoe and Mantsopa worked tirelessly, reminding them of the strength they would gain together.

However, in the shadows, Mzilikazi's spies were watching. As the gathering progressed, whispers of dissent began to circulate among the ranks of the Matabele, reaching Mzilikazi himself. He would not allow this alliance to form, not without a fight.

In the dark of night, as the embers of the fire glowed softly, Moshoeshoe felt the tension of the impending storm. He knew that the confrontation was inevitable. They had chosen a path of unity, and Mzilikazi would seek to dismantle it.

As dawn broke over Thaba Bosiu, Moshoeshoe stood at the summit, the weight of his responsibilities heavy on his heart. *"We are on the brink of a new dawn,"* he whispered to the wind, *"but we must be ready to defend our dreams."*

With determination burning in his heart, he descended the mountain to prepare his people for the battles that lay ahead. Together, they would stand firm against the gathering storm.

Chapter 10: The Gathering Forces

As dawn broke over Thaba Bosiu, the atmosphere was thick with anticipation. Moshoeshoe and his allies gathered for a final council meeting before the imminent confrontation with Mzilikazi. The fire crackled at the center of their gathering, casting flickering shadows across the faces of the leaders who had come to stand beside him.

"*We must act swiftly,*" Moshoeshoe began, his voice steady. "*The alliances we have forged will be tested. Mzilikazi will not take kindly to our efforts to unite. We must prepare ourselves, both physically and mentally, for what lies ahead.*"

Mantsopa nodded, her expression serious. "*We must also prepare our people for the possibility of loss. It is essential that they understand what we fight for—our future, our identity, and the legacy we wish to leave for those who come after us.*"

The leaders murmured their agreement, a collective resolve forming within the circle. Moshoeshoe turned to each chief in turn, drawing strength from their unwavering determination. They discussed their battle plans, the strategies they would employ to maximize their chances of success.

As they finalized their preparations, word arrived that Mzilikazi was on the move. His forces were gathering, a dark wave approaching their lands with a purpose that sent a chill through the hearts of Moshoeshoe's people. The council quickly dispatched scouts to gather intelligence and report back on the size and movements of the Matabele army.

Days turned into a flurry of activity. Warriors trained rigorously, their muscles taut with anticipation. Women and children gathered supplies and fortified their homes, prepared to support their warriors however they could. The air buzzed with a mixture of fear and excitement, each heart beating in rhythm with the growing sense of purpose.

One evening, as they gathered around the fire, Moshoeshoe felt the need to remind his people of their shared mission. "*What we fight for is more than land; it is about the future we envision. A future where our children can play freely, where our culture and traditions can thrive without the threat of war. Let that vision guide us through this storm.*"

The warriors cheered, their voices rising like a chorus of thunder, echoing the strength of their conviction. As the days passed, the Matabele forces grew closer, the sounds of war drums echoing in the distance. The tension was palpable, and Moshoeshoe could feel the weight of their destiny pressing down upon him.

On the eve of the battle, he gathered his warriors and allies at the base of Thaba Bosiu, the sacred mountain that had witnessed their trials and triumphs. "*Tomorrow, we face a great challenge,*" he said, his voice steady but filled with emotion. "*But we do so not as individuals but as a united force. Each of you carries the spirit of our ancestors, the strength of our people. Together, we are unstoppable.*"

That night, as the moon hung high in the sky, Moshoeshoe walked the quiet paths of Thaba Bosiu, reflecting on the journey that had brought them to this moment. He thought of the ancestors who had guided him, the sacrifices made along the way, and the unity they had forged. He felt the land beneath his feet, the pulse of history coursing through it.

In the early hours of the morning, the sound of war horns echoed across the valley, signaling the approach of Mzilikazi's forces. Moshoeshoe gathered his warriors, their faces set with determination. "*Today, we stand firm! We fight not just for our survival but for the dreams of our people!*"

As they formed ranks, the sight of the Matabele army approaching was both daunting and invigorating. The dust kicked up by their march swirled like a storm, a reminder of the fierce battle that awaited them. Moshoeshoe stood at the forefront, his heart pounding with a mixture of fear and resolve.

The two armies clashed with a force that shook the ground, the air filled with the sounds of war cries and the clash of weapons. Moshoeshoe fought fiercely, moving among his warriors, inspiring them with his presence. The spirit of unity surged through their ranks as they pushed back against the Matabele.

In the midst of the chaos, he spotted Mzilikazi, a formidable figure rallying his warriors. "*We must confront him!*" Moshoeshoe shouted, his voice cutting through the din. With Mokhotu by his side, they surged forward, carving a path through the fray.

As they drew closer to Mzilikazi, the Matabele leader met their charge with a fierce resolve. Their eyes locked, a silent acknowledgment of the battle that had come to define them both. "*Moshoeshoe!*" Mzilikazi bellowed, his voice thunderous over the clash of battle. "You cannot hope to defeat me! This land belongs to the strong!"

"*We are stronger together!*" Moshoeshoe shouted back, his spear poised to strike. "*You may have power, but we have unity, and that is our greatest strength!*"

With that, they clashed in a furious duel, their weapons sparking as they collided. Moshoeshoe poured every ounce of strength and conviction into each strike, remembering the faces of his people, their hopes resting on his shoulders.

Around them, the battle raged on, the tides of conflict shifting as both armies fought valiantly. Moshoeshoe could feel the spirit of his ancestors guiding him, lending strength to his blows as he pushed back against Mzilikazi's ferocity.

As the sun began to set, casting a golden glow over the battlefield, it became clear that the outcome of this battle would shape the future of their people. Moshoeshoe fought with the tenacity of a lion, and as he found an opening, he aimed to disarm Mzilikazi, knowing that victory depended on more than just brute strength.

In a moment of clarity, he struck with precision, his spear finding its mark. Mzilikazi stumbled, the surprise of the moment giving Moshoeshoe the upper hand. He seized the opportunity, but instead of delivering a fatal blow, he paused, locking eyes with his rival.

"*Join us, Mzilikazi,*" Moshoeshoe implored, the weight of the moment heavy in the air. "*Together, we can build a future that honors all our people. The cycle of bloodshed must end.*"

For a heartbeat, time stood still as they stared at one another, the fate of their people hanging in the balance.

Chapter 11: The Choice of a Warrior

The battlefield was a tumult of sound and fury, the air thick with the scent of sweat and blood. As Moshoeshoe held Mzilikazi's gaze, the roar of the conflict around them faded into a distant murmur. It was a moment suspended in time, the weight of history pressing down on both men.

Mzilikazi's eyes narrowed, a mix of fury and contemplation flickering across his face. *"You think you can sway me with words? I am not one to bow to weakness!"* His voice boomed, echoing the pride of a leader accustomed to power.

"Strength is not just in power," Moshoeshoe replied, his voice calm yet resolute. *"True strength lies in the courage to unite rather than divide, to build rather than destroy. We stand on the brink of endless conflict, but we can choose a different path. Think of your people, the lives that will be lost for nothing more than pride."*

The fury in Mzilikazi's expression softened for a moment, as the weight of Moshoeshoe's words sank in. Around them, warriors clashed, the cries of battle a stark reminder of the stakes at hand. Moshoeshoe's heart raced, hoping against hope that reason could prevail over violence.

"Do you truly believe that we could stand together?" Mzilikazi's voice faltered slightly, revealing a crack in his armor of defiance. *"After all the blood we've shed?"*

"Yes," Moshoeshoe said firmly, stepping forward. *"The land cries for peace, for unity. Let us not add more blood to its soil. Together, we can create a legacy that our children will remember with pride instead of fear."*

For a moment, the tumult of the battle faded into the background, leaving only the two leaders in focus. Moshoeshoe saw the flicker of doubt in Mzilikazi's eyes, a sign that his words were finding their mark. Yet the moment was brief, for a cry rang out, shattering the silence.

"Chief! Behind you!" Mokhotu shouted, his voice slicing through the air like a blade.

Moshoeshoe spun just in time to see a Matabele warrior charging towards him, spear poised to strike. Instinct took over, and he dodged, the spear grazing his side as he turned. In a fluid motion, he retaliated, dispatching the attacker with swift precision.

"Focus!" he called back to Mzilikazi, knowing they were both caught in a web of conflict that threatened to consume them. *"This is what we must stop! This endless cycle of violence will lead to our ruin."*

But Mzilikazi's expression hardened once more, the walls of pride re-erecting around his heart. *"You speak of peace, yet you fight! You have chosen your path."*

With that, he lunged forward, and the moment of connection was lost. Their duel resumed, a fierce dance of power and strategy. Each thrust and parry was a clash of ideals as much as it was of steel. Moshoeshoe fought with the fervor of a man who carried the weight of his people's dreams, while Mzilikazi wielded the ferocity of a warrior backed into a corner.

As the battle raged on around them, Moshoeshoe saw his warriors giving their all, inspired by his resolve. He felt a surge of energy, a connection to the land and his ancestors, urging him to fight not just for victory but for a future that transcended the present conflict.

With renewed determination, he focused on the fight, weaving through the chaos, using both skill and agility to dodge blows and deliver his own. The spirit of unity surged through him, a reminder of what they were fighting for. But even as he pressed forward, he felt the strain of fatigue begin to creep into his limbs.

Then, from the corner of his eye, he noticed a group of Mzilikazi's warriors faltering, their resolve shaken as they witnessed the strength of the Basotho fighting together. It was a sign—a flicker of hope amidst the turmoil.

"Now is our chance!" he shouted, rallying his warriors. *"Show them what we fight for! Let them see the strength of unity!"*

The Basotho warriors surged with renewed vigor, pressing against the Matabele, their battle cries rising like a thunderstorm. Mzilikazi glanced at the shifting tide of his forces, confusion dawning in his eyes.

Realizing the moment was slipping away, Moshoeshoe seized the opportunity to press forward. "*Mzilikazi!*" he shouted, desperate to reach him once more. "*Your warriors are faltering! You can end this, you can lead them to a better future!*"

In that moment, as their eyes locked again, Moshoeshoe saw the faintest hint of hesitation in Mzilikazi's stance. He took a deep breath, pouring every ounce of sincerity into his next words. "*If you stand with us, we can create a kingdom that embraces all. Together, we can be the leaders our people deserve.*"

Mzilikazi's grip on his spear tightened, a flicker of uncertainty passing across his face. The sound of the battle faded into the background, leaving only the two leaders in that fragile moment of potential.

But before he could respond, a shout rang out from the Matabele ranks. A warrior, emboldened by the moment, lunged at Moshoeshoe, forcing him to defend himself. The clash jolted Mzilikazi back into the present, and the moment of possibility slipped away.

With a roar, Mzilikazi turned his attention back to the fray, his voice rising above the chaos. "*Fight! We will not bow to weakness!*"

The energy in the air shifted as the Matabele rallied, emboldened by their leader's words. The battle swelled once more, a fierce tide of conflict that surged across the landscape.

Realizing that the chance for peace had slipped away, Moshoeshoe felt a surge of determination rise within him. They would fight, yes, but they would fight for the future, not just for survival. With every warrior at his side, he pushed forward, the spirit of unity guiding him.

As the sun dipped low in the sky, casting a fiery glow over the battlefield, Moshoeshoe fought with a heart full of hope, believing still in the possibility of a new dawn. The clash of steel echoed in the air, a relentless symphony of struggle, but within it lay the seeds of a future that could emerge from the ashes of conflict.

And so, as the battle raged on, he vowed to himself and his people that whatever the outcome, they would continue to fight for unity, for the dreams that bound them together.

Chapter 12: The Crucible of Battle

The sun hung low in the sky, casting long shadows across the battlefield as Moshoeshoe pressed forward, his heart racing in time with the chaotic rhythm of war. The clash of weapons and the cries of warriors surrounded him, a symphony of conflict that echoed the struggle for survival. But within that chaos, he remained resolute, fighting not just for victory but for a vision of peace.

Each thrust of his spear was deliberate, a reflection of the hope he carried for his people. He could see Mzilikazi's forces wavering as the unity of the Basotho warriors surged around him. Their collective spirit became a force of its own, a tidal wave of determination crashing against the remnants of Mzilikazi's pride.

"*Moshoeshoe!*" Mokhotu shouted, cutting through the din as he joined his chief, panting but undeterred. "*We need to push toward the center! We can break their formation!*"

"*Lead the way!*" Moshoeshoe responded, his voice unwavering. Together, they maneuvered through the throngs of combat, each warrior's resolve feeding the fire of their collective strength.

But just as they began to turn the tide, a sharp cry rang out. Moshoeshoe turned to see one of his warriors fall, struck by an unseen enemy. Anger surged within him, and he felt a surge of adrenaline, urging him to fight harder, to protect his people at all costs.

"*Keep fighting!*" he roared, charging forward. "*We fight for our families, our future!*"

As they moved, Moshoeshoe's attention was drawn once more to Mzilikazi, who fought fiercely at the heart of the Matabele forces. The man was a whirlwind of strength, his presence commanding respect, yet Moshoeshoe sensed a flicker of uncertainty in his eyes as he looked at the faltering morale of his warriors.

Drawing on the energy of his surroundings, Moshoeshoe pressed forward, determined to confront his rival once more. "*This is not the way, Mzilikazi!*" he shouted as he fought his way through the fray. "*You do not have to lead your people to ruin!*"

Mzilikazi's gaze met his, a flash of recognition crossing the distance. "*You speak of ruin, yet you bring your own people to battle!*" he shouted back, parrying a strike aimed at him. "*You seek to destroy what I have built!*"

"*I seek to build a future for all of us!*" Moshoeshoe replied, parrying a blow from a Matabele warrior before dodging another. "*You may have power, but we have hope! We fight for a future beyond this chaos!*"

The two leaders locked eyes once more, and Moshoeshoe could see the conflict raging within Mzilikazi. But before he could reach him again, a group of Matabele surged forward, forcing him to focus on the battle once more.

As the clash of steel echoed around them, Moshoeshoe fought with a fire fueled by the dreams of his people. Every strike was a reminder of the families waiting for their warriors to return, of the legacy they were forging together.

Gradually, the tide began to shift. The Basotho's resolve strengthened, the warriors fighting with an unyielding spirit. They pressed forward, pushing against Mzilikazi's forces, their shouts of unity rising above the cacophony of battle.

Yet even as victory seemed within reach, the battlefield was a brutal crucible. Moshoeshoe could feel the toll of the fight taking its due. His muscles burned, and he could see fatigue etched into the faces of his warriors. The relentless combat tested their resolve, but they pressed on, fueled by the dream of a united future.

As the sun dipped below the horizon, casting an eerie glow over the battlefield, the sounds of battle began to shift. The Matabele forces, sensing the growing strength of the Basotho, began to falter. Mzilikazi's roar of command was met with uncertainty, and Moshoeshoe seized the moment.

"*Now!*" he shouted, rallying his warriors. "*For our future! For unity!*"

With a united cry, the Basotho surged forward, pushing back against the Matabele lines. Moshoeshoe fought alongside them, his spear cutting through the chaos, each movement a testament to the vision that had brought them together.

But just as victory seemed certain, a piercing scream shattered the air. Moshoeshoe's heart dropped as he turned to see Mantsopa, her figure illuminated by the flickering flames of battle, surrounded by Matabele warriors. She fought valiantly, but the odds were against her.

"*Mantsopa!*" he cried, desperation fueling his charge.

With a renewed urgency, he broke free from the fray, carving a path toward her. He could see the determination in her eyes, but also the struggle as she fought to fend off her attackers. As he closed the distance, he unleashed a flurry of strikes, his spear finding its mark against the Matabele forces.

"*Mantsopa, stay close!*" he urged, cutting down an attacker who sought to close in on her.

"*Moshoeshoe, we need to regroup!*" she shouted, her voice filled with both urgency and strength. "*We can't let them isolate us!*"

Together, they fought side by side, their movements synchronized as they carved through the chaos. Moshoeshoe felt a surge of gratitude; her presence at his side was a reminder of the unity they were fighting to protect.

As they fought back to back, the tide of battle began to shift once more. The Matabele forces, sensing their leaders' faltering grip on the fight, began to retreat. Moshoeshoe felt a flicker of hope, but it was tempered by the awareness of the cost of this conflict.

"*Together, we can win this!*" he urged Mantsopa, who nodded, determination etched on her face.

With renewed purpose, they pushed forward, driving the Matabele back. The cries of victory began to rise as warriors from both sides witnessed the resolve of the Basotho. One by one, the Matabele began to falter, their formation breaking under the weight of their own uncertainty.

"*Now is our moment!*" Moshoeshoe shouted, rallying his warriors for one final charge. "*For our people! For unity!*"

With a collective roar, the Basotho surged forward, their spirits unyielding as they pressed against the Matabele. The sun dipped low, casting a warm glow over the battlefield, illuminating the fierce determination in their eyes.

As the final clash echoed through the valley, Moshoeshoe fought with a fire that could not be extinguished. Each strike was a step toward a future where their dreams could take root, where unity could flourish.

And as the last remnants of the Matabele forces fell back, a sense of hope began to take hold. The battlefield was littered with the evidence of their struggle, but amid the chaos, the spirit of unity burned brighter than ever.

As Moshoeshoe stood, surrounded by his warriors, he knew this was only the beginning. The path to peace would be fraught with challenges, but today, they had taken a vital step forward.

In that moment, he turned to Mantsopa, gratitude flooding through him. "We did this together," he said, his voice steady. "*This victory belongs to all of us.*"

Her smile was fierce, a reflection of the unwavering spirit they had fought for. "*And it is a step toward a greater future.*"

As the sun set on the horizon, casting the battlefield in shades of gold and crimson, Moshoeshoe felt the weight of their victory—a victory not just over an enemy, but a victory for hope, for dreams, and for unity.

Chapter 13: The Aftermath

As the last echoes of battle faded into the twilight, the reality of their victory began to settle over the field. The cries of the wounded mingled with the soft whispers of the evening breeze, creating a haunting melody that spoke of both triumph and loss. Moshoeshoe surveyed the scene, his heart heavy with the weight of what had transpired.

Around him, his warriors tended to their fallen comrades, a solemn duty that contrasted sharply with the exhilaration of their hard-won victory. The ground was littered with remnants of the fierce struggle—shattered shields, discarded weapons, and the fallen, each a reminder of the price paid for their freedom.

"Mantsopa," he called, searching for her a midst the chaos. She emerged from the shadows, her face marked with the grime of battle, but her eyes shone with determination.

"We did it, Moshoeshoe," she said, her voice filled with a mix of exhaustion and relief. *"But at what cost?"*

The question hung heavy between them, a truth they could not ignore. *"We must honor those we've lost,"* he replied, his voice steady but tinged with sorrow. *"Their sacrifice cannot be in vain. We must ensure that this victory leads to something greater."*

As they moved through the aftermath, Moshoeshoe took note of the wounded, both Basotho and Matabele. It was a sight that filled him with a sense of responsibility. He called for the healers among his people, directing them to tend to the injured, regardless of their allegiance.

"We are not conquerors; we are leaders," he proclaimed. *"We will show compassion even to those who stood against us. Let us be a light in this darkness."*

The healers set to work, their hands skilled and steady as they tended to the wounds. Moshoeshoe observed, feeling a sense of pride swell within him. This act of kindness would echo far beyond the battlefield, planting seeds of understanding and reconciliation.

"Mantsopa," he said, turning to her. *"We need to send word to the Matabele leaders. They must know that we seek peace, not further conflict. This cycle of violence has to end."*

She nodded, her expression resolute. *"I will gather our fastest runners. We must reach them before they can regroup."*

As she moved to organize the messengers, Moshoeshoe felt a renewed sense of purpose. The battle had shown him that the spirit of unity was stronger than the forces that sought to divide them. But the challenge ahead was daunting. Mzilikazi remained a formidable leader, and the scars of this conflict would linger.

Night fell, cloaking the battlefield in shadows. The air was heavy with the weight of unspoken words, and Moshoeshoe found himself reflecting on the confrontation with Mzilikazi. Had he made the right choice in showing mercy? The answer lay not in the heat of battle but in the aftermath, in how they would rebuild and forge a new path together.

As dawn broke over the horizon, a new day brought clarity. The wounded were being cared for, and whispers of hope began to circulate among his people. Moshoeshoe called for a gathering at the base of Thaba Bosiu, the sacred mountain that had been their refuge.

Warriors and villagers assembled, their faces marked with the remnants of battle yet glowing with the spirit of survival. Moshoeshoe stood before them, Mantsopa at his side, and spoke with conviction.

"Today, we honor those we have lost," he began, his voice carrying across the crowd. *"Their bravery will not be forgotten. This victory is not merely ours; it is a testament to the strength of our unity. We must carry this spirit forward."*

The crowd murmured in agreement, their resolve strengthening with each word. *"But we also must seek peace with those who fought against us. I call upon the Matabele to join us in rebuilding, to work together toward a future where our children can grow without the shadow of war."*

A hush fell over the crowd, a mix of hope and uncertainty hanging in the air. Moshoeshoe could sense the weight of their history—the bitterness of conflict ran deep, but so too did the desire for a better tomorrow.

"*Mantsopa,*" he said, turning to her, "*please share your vision for our future.*"

She stepped forward, her presence commanding as she addressed the crowd. "*Together, we can forge a new path, one that honors our ancestors and embraces our shared humanity. We must work toward unity, not just in our own communities but with our neighbors as well. The time has come to build alliances that will stand the test of time.*"

Her words resonated deeply, igniting a flicker of hope among the crowd. Moshoeshoe watched as the warriors nodded, their expressions shifting from weariness to determination.

"*And in this effort, we will not shy away from our past,*" Mantsopa continued. "*We will remember the lessons learned in battle, the sacrifices made, and let those guide our future.*"

With a renewed sense of purpose, the crowd erupted in cheers, their voices a chorus of hope that echoed across the valley. Moshoeshoe felt a swell of pride and gratitude. Together, they were more than just a collection of warriors; they were a community united in their vision for the future.

As the sun rose higher in the sky, illuminating the landscape with its golden light, Moshoeshoe knew that their journey was far from over. The path ahead would be filled with challenges, but they would face them together. The strength of unity, once forged in battle, would become their guiding light.

And as he looked out over the faces of his people, he felt the weight of their dreams resting on his shoulders—a burden he would carry with honor.

Chapter 14: The Call to Unity

In the days that followed the battle, a palpable sense of change filled the air. The sun rose with a renewed brilliance, casting light on the lands that had witnessed so much strife. Moshoeshoe and his people worked tirelessly, not just to heal the wounds of war but to lay the groundwork for a future built on the principles of cooperation and understanding.

Messages were sent to Mzilikazi and the Matabele, extending a hand of peace. Moshoeshoe understood that rebuilding trust would be a slow process, but he was resolute in his belief that it was essential for their survival.

As the weeks passed, Mantsopa organized meetings with community leaders from both sides. They gathered at Thaba Bosiu, a neutral ground where discussions could flourish away from the echoes of past conflicts. The mountain stood as a silent witness, a reminder of the unity and resilience of the Basotho people.

During one such gathering, Moshoeshoe stood at the forefront, flanked by Mantsopa and other leaders. The atmosphere buzzed with a mix of hope and skepticism as representatives from the Matabele arrived, their expressions guarded.

"Welcome," Moshoeshoe began, his voice steady and warm. *"We gather here today not as enemies, but as people who seek a new path forward. The battle we fought was fierce, but it taught us the value of unity."*

Mzilikazi stepped forward, his presence commanding despite the tension in the air. *"You speak of unity, Moshoeshoe, but the wounds of battle run deep. How can we trust that this is not just a façade?"*

"Trust is earned," Moshoeshoe replied, meeting Mzilikazi's gaze with unwavering sincerity. *"But we must start somewhere. Let us build bridges instead of walls. Together, we can cultivate the land, share resources, and create a future where our children can thrive in peace."*

The murmurs among the assembled leaders grew, some nodding in agreement while others remained skeptical. Moshoeshoe felt the weight of their gazes, the hopes and fears of both his people and the Matabele resting on this moment.

"Mantsopa has a vision for how we can move forward," he continued, gesturing to her. *"She understands the power of collaboration."*

Mantsopa stepped forward, her eyes scanning the crowd. *"We stand at a crossroads. The choice is ours to make. We can continue to allow our past to dictate our future, or we can forge a new narrative—one that includes all of us."*

Her words resonated deeply, and Moshoeshoe could see the shift in the room. Hesitation began to melt away, replaced by a collective curiosity about what a united future might look like.

"We can share knowledge, trade goods, and support each other's communities," Mantsopa added, her voice strong and passionate. *"Imagine a land where our peoples work side by side, not as enemies, but as allies."*

Mzilikazi seemed to consider her words carefully, the tension in his shoulders slowly easing. *"You speak of collaboration as if it's easy, but the pain of our losses still lingers. How do we heal those wounds?"*

"By acknowledging them," Moshoeshoe replied, stepping back in. *"We must remember our history, but we cannot allow it to define us. We can honor those who fell by creating a legacy of peace in their name."*

A silence enveloped the gathering as leaders absorbed his words. One elder from the Matabele stepped forward, his face etched with lines of age and wisdom. *"It is a brave proposition you make, Moshoeshoe. But what will you offer in return for our trust?"*

"Let us start with a pact," Moshoeshoe suggested, his heart racing. *"A commitment to share resources and protect one another. We will form a council—representatives from both our peoples—to ensure that grievances are addressed and peace is upheld."*

Mzilikazi regarded Moshoeshoe thoughtfully. *"And if this council fails? If old grievances resurface?"*

"*Then we will address them openly,*" Moshoeshoe said, a spark of determination igniting within him. "*We will not shy away from conflict; instead, we will face it with courage and transparency. It is time for a new way of leading—a way that values dialogue over violence.*"

After a lengthy silence, Mzilikazi nodded slowly, the weight of his decision clear in his eyes. "*I am willing to consider your proposal, but I will not make promises lightly. Trust will take time.*"

Moshoeshoe felt a surge of hope. "*That is all we ask. Let us walk this path together, one step at a time.*"

As the discussions continued, Moshoeshoe sensed a shift in the atmosphere. The weight of skepticism began to lift, replaced by a cautious optimism. Ideas flowed freely, and a vision for their shared future started to take shape.

The gathering concluded with a commitment to meet again in a fortnight, each side tasked with selecting representatives for the new council. Moshoeshoe and Mantsopa left the meeting feeling a renewed sense of purpose, hopeful that they had taken a significant step toward healing.

As they walked back to their camp, the sun setting behind them, casting a golden hue over the land, Moshoeshoe turned to Mantsopa. "*Today was a pivotal moment. I can feel the tide turning.*"

"*It is just the beginning,*" she replied, her expression thoughtful. "*We must remain vigilant, but there is a spark of hope. If we can foster this unity, our people will thrive.*"

"*Together, we can reshape our destinies,*" Moshoeshoe said, determination echoing in his voice. "*We will build a legacy that honors our past while paving the way for future generations.*"

As they continued their journey, Moshoeshoe felt the weight of history on his shoulders, but also a lightness in his heart. They were forging a new path, one that held the promise of unity, hope, and a future where all could flourish together.

Chapter 15: The Council of Elders

The days leading up to the council meeting were filled with a mix of anticipation and anxiety. Moshoeshoe and Mantsopa worked tirelessly to prepare their people for this significant step toward unity. News of the proposed council spread through the Basotho and Matabele communities, stirring hope but also apprehension.

On the morning of the meeting, Moshoeshoe stood at the foot of Thaba Bosiu, gazing at the mountain that had long served as a symbol of strength and refuge. Today, it would witness a pivotal moment in their shared history.

As the sun climbed higher, illuminating the landscape, representatives from both sides began to arrive. The atmosphere buzzed with nervous energy; warriors, elders, and leaders gathered in a clearing, each one carrying the weight of their people's hopes and fears.

Mantsopa stood beside him, her presence a calming force. *"Remember, we are here to listen as much as we are to speak,"* she reminded him, her voice steady.

Moshoeshoe nodded, knowing that patience would be key. As the last of the representatives settled in, he stepped forward, taking a deep breath to steady himself. *"Welcome, friends and leaders,"* he began, his voice carrying across the clearing. *"We gather here today not as adversaries, but as people who seek to build a future together."*

The crowd fell silent, all eyes on him. *"We have come through a storm, and though the scars remain, it is time to lay the foundation for a new beginning. Today, we will establish a council—a place for dialogue, a bridge over the chasm that divides us."*

Mantsopa stepped forward, her gaze sweeping across the faces of both Basotho and Matabele. *"Our aim is to ensure that every voice is heard. Each grievance addressed. Together, we can forge a path toward understanding."*

The Matabele representatives, led by an elder named Ngwenya, exchanged glances, uncertainty etched on their faces. *"And what assurance do we have that this council will bring true change?"* Ngwenya asked, his voice steady but cautious.

"Change begins with us," Moshoeshoe replied, his tone earnest. *"We must commit to transparency and honesty. We will document our discussions and decisions, holding each other accountable."*

Ngwenya nodded slowly, seemingly contemplating the proposition. *"We have lost much, and trust will not come easily. But perhaps this is a step worth taking."*

With a collective breath, the council members began to introduce themselves, sharing stories of loss and hope. Moshoeshoe listened intently, his heart heavy with the weight of their shared histories. He sensed the pain in their words, a testament to the lives affected by their conflict.

As the meeting progressed, discussions turned toward practical matters. They debated how to share resources, manage disputes, and collaborate on agricultural projects that could benefit both communities.

Moshoeshoe proposed a festival—a celebration of their shared heritage, where stories could be exchanged and relationships nurtured. *"Let us honor our ancestors together,"* he suggested. *"A time to remember what we have lost and celebrate what we can achieve together."*

The idea sparked enthusiasm among the members. Mantsopa elaborated on the concept, suggesting that the festival could include cultural exchanges, where the Basotho and Matabele could share their traditions through dance, music, and food.

Slowly, the tension in the air began to dissipate, replaced by a growing sense of camaraderie. Laughter and spirited discussions filled the clearing as representatives from both sides engaged with one another, sharing ideas and insights.

Yet, amid the budding optimism, Moshoeshoe remained acutely aware of the fractures still present. Not everyone was convinced of the council's potential. As the meeting drew to a close, he sensed lingering doubts in some hearts.

"Change is a journey," he reminded them, his voice firm yet compassionate. *"We will face challenges along the way. But if we are united in purpose, we can overcome them together."*

As the sun began to set, casting a warm glow over the gathering, the council members pledged to meet regularly, committing to nurturing the fragile bonds being formed. They agreed on the festival's date, and plans began to take shape.

As they dispersed, Moshoeshoe and Mantsopa lingered for a moment, exchanging hopeful glances. "*Today felt like a turning point,*" she said, her voice filled with cautious optimism.

"*It is just the beginning,*" he replied, feeling the weight of their shared responsibility. "*But if we can foster this spirit of cooperation, we can change the course of our history.*"

As they walked away from the gathering, the air around them crackled with the promise of a new era. The journey ahead would not be easy, but together they would face whatever challenges lay in wait. The seeds of unity had been planted, and with patience and determination, they would grow into something beautiful.

Chapter 16: The Festival of Unity

The day of the festival dawned bright and clear, the sun casting a warm glow over the landscape. The air was thick with anticipation, as the Basotho and Matabele communities gathered at Thaba Bosiu to celebrate their shared heritage and newfound alliance. Colorful banners adorned the pathways, and the sound of laughter and music filled the air.

Moshoeshoe and Mantsopa arrived early, overseeing the preparations. Tables laden with food, traditional dishes from both cultures, stood ready to welcome guests. The aroma of stews, roasted meats, and baked goods wafted through the air, stirring appetites and memories of communal feasts past.

"Look at this," Mantsopa said, her eyes sparkling as she gestured to the decorations. *"It's beautiful. This festival can truly be a bridge between our peoples."*

Moshoeshoe nodded, a sense of pride swelling within him. *"Today, we celebrate not just our cultures, but our shared future. Let us show our communities what unity looks like."*

As the sun rose higher, people began to arrive, warriors in their traditional attire mingling with families and children. The festival grounds buzzed with energy, and Moshoeshoe felt a wave of hope wash over him. This was more than just a celebration; it was a manifestation of their collective dreams.

Soon, the festivities commenced. Moshoeshoe welcomed the crowd, his voice rising above the cheerful din. *"Today, we come together to honor our ancestors and to build a future filled with hope and understanding. Let us embrace our differences and celebrate what unites us!"*

The crowd erupted in applause, their cheers echoing across the valley. Mantsopa took her place beside him, ready to lead the first dance. As the drummers began to play, the rhythmic beats resonated through the ground, inviting everyone to join in.

Men and women from both communities danced together, laughter and joy mingling in the air. Moshoeshoe watched as the barriers of mistrust began to crumble, replaced by a spirit of camaraderie. Children from both sides ran and played, their laughter a harmonious reminder of the innocence they sought to protect.

As the day wore on, stories were shared—tales of bravery, love, and resilience. Elders exchanged wisdom, while younger generations listened with wide eyes, soaking in the rich history that bound them all.

During a quiet moment, Mantsopa approached Moshoeshoe, her expression thoughtful. *"Do you think we can maintain this spirit of unity after today?"*

Moshoeshoe met her gaze, feeling the weight of the question. *"I believe we can, but it will require commitment. The council must continue to foster these connections. We must keep the lines of communication open."*

"Agreed," she said, determination shining in her eyes. *"Today is a step, but it's up to us to guide our people forward."*

As the sun began to set, painting the sky in hues of orange and purple, the festival reached its climax. Performers from both sides took the stage, showcasing traditional dances, songs, and stories that celebrated their shared heritage.

Moshoeshoe and Mantsopa stood together, watching as the energy of the crowd swelled. It was a sight that filled him with hope—a tangible manifestation of their hard work and commitment to unity.

Just as the final performance concluded, a hush fell over the crowd. Moshoeshoe took a deep breath, sensing the significance of the moment. *"Let us light this fire together,"* he said, motioning to a large bonfire prepared at the center of the gathering. *"This fire will symbolize our unity and the warmth of our newfound friendship."*

He and Mantsopa moved to ignite the flames, the flickering light illuminating their faces. As the fire blazed to life, cheers erupted from the crowd, voices rising in celebration.

"This fire represents our commitment to one another," Moshoeshoe declared, his voice steady. *"May it burn brightly as a reminder of the bonds we've formed here today."*

As night descended, the festival transformed into a magical gathering of light and warmth. The crackling fire drew people closer, and the music played late into the evening. Stories flowed, laughter echoed, and the spirit of unity enveloped them all.

As the festivities began to wind down, Moshoeshoe felt a sense of fulfillment wash over him. He knew that the journey ahead would not be without its challenges, but today marked a pivotal moment—a beacon of hope in a world that had known too much strife.

In that moment, he turned to Mantsopa, who was smiling as she watched the gathering. "*We did this together,*" he said, gratitude evident in his voice.

She nodded, her eyes reflecting the light of the fire. "*And this is only the beginning. We must keep nurturing this spirit.*"

"*Together, we will,*" Moshoeshoe vowed, feeling the warmth of her presence beside him. They stood together, united in their vision for the future, ready to face whatever challenges lay ahead.

Chapter 17: Shadows of Doubt

In the weeks following the festival, the spirit of unity continued to blossom within the communities of the Basotho and Matabele. The council convened regularly, discussions filled with a renewed sense of purpose. However, a midst the joy and collaboration, shadows of doubt lingered in some hearts, threatening to undermine their progress.

Moshoeshoe often found himself reflecting on the challenges that lay ahead. Though the festival had ignited hope, he knew that true change would require constant vigilance and effort. He gathered his closest advisors at Thaba Bosiu to address the lingering concerns.

"Mantsopa," he began, as they sat in a circle, the sun filtering through the trees above, *"what are we hearing from the council? Are the voices of dissent still present?"*

Mantsopa nodded, her expression serious. *"Yes, there are those who doubt our intentions. Some believe that this council is merely a façade—a way to pacify them while we strengthen our own power."*

"We must address these fears openly," Moshoeshoe said, his brow furrowing. *"If we allow mistrust to fester, we risk everything we have built."*

An elder named Khotso, a trusted advisor, spoke up. *"Perhaps we should hold another gathering—this time, a forum specifically for those who feel marginalized. We need to listen to their grievances and show that their voices matter."*

Moshoeshoe considered this suggestion carefully. *"That could be a way to bridge the gap. If we acknowledge their concerns, it may help foster a greater sense of belonging."*

Mantsopa leaned in, her eyes brightening. *"We can invite those who were skeptical at the festival. A forum that encourages dialogue and understanding could be a powerful tool for healing."*

With a renewed sense of purpose, the group set about planning the forum. They would invite not only the leaders but also members from both communities who had reservations about the council's intentions.

As the days passed, word of the upcoming forum spread throughout the communities. Moshoeshoe felt a mix of anticipation and anxiety as the date approached. Would they be able to address the doubts that lingered?

On the day of the forum, tension filled the air as people gathered at Thaba Bosiu once more. Moshoeshoe could see the skepticism etched on some faces, the wounds of the past still fresh. He and Mantsopa stood at the forefront, ready to guide the discussions.

As the forum began, Moshoeshoe welcomed everyone, acknowledging the courage it took to share their concerns. *"Today, we come together not just as leaders, but as fellow community members. Your voices matter, and we are here to listen."*

The crowd murmured, a mix of uncertainty and hope. He could sense the weight of their collective history pressing down on them, but he also felt the potential for understanding in the air.

A woman named Thandi, representing the Matabele, spoke first. *"We have lost much, and our trust has been shattered. How can we believe that this council truly seeks our good?"*

Moshoeshoe listened intently, the honesty in her voice striking a chord within him. *"Your pain is valid, Thandi. We cannot erase the past, but we can strive for a future where we support one another. We must work together to rebuild what has been broken."*

Another voice rose from the crowd, a Basotho man named Lekoa. *"We have fought for our land, our people. How do we know that sharing with the Matabele won't lead to further loss?"*

Mantsopa stepped forward, her voice steady. *"I understand your fears, Lekoa. But consider this: when we work together, we can cultivate strength. We can protect our lands as allies, rather than enemies."*

As the discussions continued, it became clear that many were yearning for a dialogue that acknowledged their pain while offering a path forward. Moshoeshoe facilitated the conversation, encouraging everyone to share their stories, their grievances, and their hopes.

Gradually, the atmosphere began to shift. Skepticism gave way to a cautious openness. Moshoeshoe could see the walls beginning to crumble as people engaged with one another, their shared humanity becoming evident.

By the end of the forum, they had established a plan for ongoing communication, a commitment to meet regularly and address any grievances as they arose. The act of listening had proven powerful, forging connections that had previously felt impossible.

As the crowd began to disperse, Moshoeshoe felt a sense of relief wash over him. They had faced the shadows of doubt head-on, and while challenges still lay ahead, he believed they had taken a significant step toward healing.

"Mantsopa," he said, turning to her, *"today was a turning point. We showed that our intentions are sincere."*

"It was a necessary step," she replied, her eyes sparkling with determination. *"But we must remain vigilant. There will always be those who resist change."*

"I know," he said, his voice resolute. *"But as long as we listen and engage, we can build a future where everyone feels they belong."*

As they walked away from the gathering, Moshoeshoe felt a renewed sense of hope. The journey ahead would be difficult, but he was no longer walking alone. Together, they would navigate the complexities of their shared history, fostering a spirit of unity that could withstand the test of time.

Chapter 18: A Gathering Storm

The months that followed the forum saw both progress and setbacks. The council convened regularly, and while many voices were heard, lingering tensions remained. Moshoeshoe often found himself reflecting on the delicate balance they were striving to maintain. Unity was a fragile thread, easily frayed by the winds of doubt and resentment.

As the dry season approached, the landscape around Thaba Bosiu grew parched, and the once-vibrant colors faded into muted browns and yellows. The struggle for resources intensified, and whispers of discontent began to circulate once more.

One evening, as Moshoeshoe reviewed reports from the council, a messenger arrived, breathless and urgent. *"Chief, there are rumors of unrest among the Matabele. Some warriors are gathering near the border, claiming they want to protect their lands."*

Moshoeshoe's heart sank. *"Who is leading them?"*

"Some say it is a young warrior named Sizwe, who believes that the council has betrayed their trust," the messenger replied, concern etched on his face.

Mantsopa entered the room just then, sensing the tension in the air. *"What news?"*

"Trouble brews among the Matabele," Moshoeshoe said, his voice grave. *"We must act quickly to prevent conflict. This could undermine everything we have worked for."*

"We need to address Sizwe directly," Mantsopa suggested. *"If we can engage him in dialogue, we may be able to quell the unrest before it escalates."*

With resolve, Moshoeshoe gathered a small group of trusted advisors and set out to meet with Sizwe. They traveled to the border, where the tension in the air was palpable. As they approached the gathering of warriors, Moshoeshoe felt a mixture of apprehension and determination.

Sizwe stood at the forefront, his presence commanding as he addressed his fellow warriors. *"We cannot stand idly by while our lands are threatened! The council speaks of unity, but we know the truth. We have lost much already!"*

Moshoeshoe stepped forward, raising his hand to signal for calm. *"Sizwe, I am here to listen. I understand your concerns, but violence is not the answer."*

The young warrior's eyes blazed with intensity. *"How can you speak of peace when we see our lands dry up, our resources dwindling? What has the council done for us?"*

Mantsopa joined Moshoeshoe, her voice steady. *"We are aware of the struggles you face. The drought affects us all, and it is through cooperation that we can find solutions. Fighting amongst ourselves will only lead to greater suffering."*

Sizwe's expression softened momentarily, but doubt lingered. *"And how can we trust that the council will not prioritize the Basotho over us? We have been burned before."*

Moshoeshoe felt the weight of his words. *"I cannot change the past, but I can promise you this: we are committed to working together. We have resources that we can share, and through collaboration, we can weather this storm."*

"Prove it," Sizwe challenged, his tone defiant. *"Show us that you will not abandon your promises."*

With the crowd's attention focused on him, Moshoeshoe knew this was a pivotal moment. *"Then let us gather our people—Basotho and Matabele alike. We can host a joint meeting to address these concerns directly. Together, we can develop a plan to manage our resources and support one another through this drought."*

The murmurs among the warriors indicated a shift in the atmosphere. Sizwe's gaze remained skeptical, but the flicker of hope was unmistakable. *"I will bring my people to this meeting,"* he finally said. *"But you must ensure that our voices are heard."*

Moshoeshoe nodded, relief flooding through him. *"You have my word. Together, we will find a way forward."*

As they returned to Thaba Bosiu, Moshoeshoe felt a renewed sense of urgency. This meeting would be critical in determining the future of their alliance. He and Mantsopa spent the following days preparing, reaching out to both communities, urging them to come together once more.

On the day of the meeting, the atmosphere was electric with tension. People from both sides gathered, wary but hopeful. Moshoeshoe stood at the forefront, flanked by Sizwe and Mantsopa, ready to address the crowd.

"Today, we stand together at a crossroads," he began, his voice steady. *"The drought affects us all, and we must find a way to support one another through this challenge. Our strength lies in our unity."*

As he spoke, he could see the skepticism in some faces, but also a flicker of hope. Mantsopa stepped forward to emphasize the importance of collaboration, and Sizwe, although still cautious, echoed her sentiments, urging the crowd to share their concerns openly.

Throughout the meeting, voices rose and fell, ideas exchanged, and tensions slowly eased. They discussed ways to share water sources, implement sustainable farming practices, and develop community support systems.

Moshoeshoe could sense the shift in the room; the walls of mistrust were slowly crumbling as dialogue replaced hostility.

As the meeting concluded, Moshoeshoe felt a sense of accomplishment wash over him. They had faced the storm together, and while challenges remained, they had taken significant steps toward unity.

Yet, deep down, he knew that the path ahead would be fraught with difficulties. The drought was relentless, and not everyone would be satisfied with their decisions.

As he walked home with Mantsopa by his side, he couldn't shake the feeling that a greater challenge loomed on the horizon, one that would test their resolve and commitment to unity.

"Do you think we can sustain this momentum?" Mantsopa asked, concern flickering in her eyes.

"With patience and perseverance, I believe we can," he replied, though doubt lingered in his heart. *"But we must remain vigilant. Our greatest tests are yet to come."*

Chapter 19: The Test of Unity

As the dry season deepened, the impact of the drought became more pronounced. The rivers that had once flowed with life now trickled weakly, and the fields lay parched, their promise of abundance diminished. The unity forged at the recent meetings was put to the test as desperation began to creep into the hearts of both communities.

Moshoeshoe and Mantsopa met regularly to strategize and monitor the situation. The council had created task forces to address resource distribution, but whispers of discontent began to echo through the villages. Skepticism lingered, and rumors spread that the Matabele were receiving preferential treatment.

One evening, as they reviewed reports in the council chamber, a delegation from the Basotho arrived, their expressions grave. The leader, an elder named Teboho, stepped forward, his voice filled with concern. *"Chief Moshoeshoe, the people are restless. They believe that the Matabele are taking more than their share. We need to address this before it escalates into conflict."*

Moshoeshoe felt a tightening in his chest. *"We are all suffering,"* he replied. *"It is crucial that we communicate openly. We must reassure our people that resources are being shared fairly."*

Mantsopa nodded, her gaze steady. *"Perhaps another gathering is in order—an opportunity for both sides to voice their concerns and reaffirm our commitment to unity."*

Moshoeshoe agreed, though he sensed the rising tension. The next gathering would need to address not just the distribution of resources but also the growing distrust among the Basotho.

On the day of the gathering, the atmosphere was heavy with anticipation. Moshoeshoe stood before a large crowd, flanked by Mantsopa and Sizwe, who had now become an essential ally in the council. The tension was palpable, and Moshoeshoe could see the apprehension etched on the faces of his people.

"Friends, we gather here today in a time of trial," he began, his voice firm yet compassionate. *"The drought has tested our resolve and our commitment to one another. We must remember that our strength lies in unity."*

A murmur rippled through the crowd, but some voices rose in protest. *"What about fairness?"* a Basotho woman called out. *"We are losing our livelihoods while the Matabele seem to thrive!"*

Moshoeshoe raised his hands for calm. *"I understand your concerns. We must address this openly. Sizwe, please share your perspective."*

Sizwe stepped forward, addressing the crowd with honesty. *"We are all suffering. The drought affects both our communities, and it is essential that we share our resources equally. I urge you to trust that our council is committed to fairness."*

Despite his words, tension simmered just beneath the surface. A young Basotho warrior stood up, anger flashing in his eyes. *"Trust? How can we trust when our lands dry up while you take from our rivers?"*

Mantsopa interjected, her voice calm yet firm. *"This council was created to protect all our interests. We must work together, not as enemies, but as allies. If we allow mistrust to divide us, we will only deepen our suffering."*

The dialogue continued, and while some voices sought to escalate the conflict, others called for unity. Slowly, the crowd began to engage in meaningful discussions, sharing ideas on resource management and support systems.

As the gathering wore on, Moshoeshoe felt a glimmer of hope. They were navigating through the storm of discontent, working to bridge the gaps. But as evening approached, he sensed that the true test of their unity was still to come.

Just as the meeting was concluding, a commotion erupted at the edge of the gathering. A group of young Basotho warriors stormed forward, their faces fierce with anger.

"Enough of this talk!" one of them shouted. *"We are tired of sharing our water and our land! It's time to take back what is ours!"*

Moshoeshoe's heart raced as he recognized the danger of the moment. "*Hold on!*" he called out, raising his hand. "*This is not the way. We must find a solution together, not through violence.*"

But the young warrior, emboldened by anger, shouted back, "*You have betrayed us! We will not stand by while our families suffer!*"

Sizwe stepped forward, his voice strong. "*This is not the answer. We need to unite, not divide. Do you want to see our people fight amongst themselves?*"

The tension crackled like a live wire, and Moshoeshoe stepped closer to the agitated warriors, seeking to connect with them. "*I understand your pain. We are all suffering, and anger is a natural response. But violence will only lead to more suffering for everyone. We cannot afford to let our emotions cloud our judgment.*"

The young warriors hesitated, caught between their anger and the truth of Moshoeshoe's words. Mantsopa moved forward, her voice soothing. "*Let us work together to find a way forward. We are stronger united than divided by fear and mistrust.*"

Gradually, the warriors began to lower their weapons, uncertainty etched on their faces. Moshoeshoe sensed the shift, and he pressed on. "*Let us commit to addressing your concerns—together. We will hold another forum, focused solely on resource management, where every voice will be heard.*"

After a tense moment, the warriors nodded reluctantly, the fire in their eyes dimming. "*We will give you one more chance,*" the young warrior said, his voice still defiant but tinged with uncertainty.

Moshoeshoe felt a wave of relief wash over him, but he knew that this was merely a temporary reprieve. The challenges they faced were far from over, and their journey toward unity remained fraught with obstacles.

As the gathering dispersed, he turned to Mantsopa and Sizwe, his expression serious. "*We must act swiftly to demonstrate our commitment to fairness. If we do not address their concerns, we risk losing everything.*"

Mantsopa nodded, her determination unwavering. "*Together, we will find a way. But we must also prepare for the possibility that not everyone will agree.*"

As they made their way home, Moshoeshoe felt the weight of the world pressing on his shoulders. The storm of doubt still loomed large, but he held onto the belief that through courage, compassion, and collaboration, they could weather any tempest that lay ahead.

Chapter 20: The Forum of Resolve

The days leading up to the next forum were a whirlwind of preparations. Moshoeshoe, Mantsopa, and Sizwe worked tirelessly to ensure that the concerns of both the Basotho and Matabele were addressed. Flyers were distributed, invitations sent, and hopes ignited once more.

As the day of the forum arrived, the atmosphere was charged with anticipation. People gathered at Thaba Bosiu, some with apprehension, others with cautious hope. The sun shone brightly overhead, but the undercurrents of tension were palpable.

Moshoeshoe stood at the forefront, flanked by Mantsopa and Sizwe. *"Thank you all for coming,"* he began, his voice steady. *"We gather here today not just to address our challenges, but to reaffirm our commitment to each other as neighbors and allies."*

A murmur of acknowledgment rippled through the crowd, though skepticism lingered in some eyes. He could sense that trust was fragile, hanging by a thread.

"Today, we will hear from both sides," Moshoeshoe continued. *"I urge you to speak openly. Let us find common ground and solutions that benefit all our people."*

He gestured to a table set up for representatives from both communities, where individuals could share their stories and concerns. The first speaker, a Matabele elder named Nkosi, stepped forward.

"The drought has affected us all," Nkosi began, his voice strong yet resonating with the weight of his years. *"But we must ensure that resources are shared equitably. We cannot let fear dictate our actions. We need a plan that supports every family, regardless of background."*

The crowd murmured in agreement, and Moshoeshoe felt a flicker of hope. It was a reminder that many shared his vision for unity.

A young Basotho woman stood next, her hands trembling slightly. *"My family has suffered greatly. We have lost crops and livestock. How can we trust that the council will protect our interests?"*

Sizwe stepped up, addressing her directly. *"Your pain is valid, and we are here to listen. We cannot change the past, but we can commit to a future where every voice matters."*

As the forum progressed, more people shared their concerns. Tensions simmered, but they also ignited discussions about practical solutions. Water-sharing agreements, cooperative farming initiatives, and communal aid efforts began to take shape.

Yet, as the discussions unfolded, a familiar voice rose above the crowd—a young warrior from the earlier gathering. *"Words are not enough! We need action! If the council cannot guarantee our livelihoods, we will take matters into our own hands!"*

A wave of unrest spread through the crowd, and Moshoeshoe felt the familiar tightening in his chest. He stepped forward, raising his hands for calm. *"I understand your frustration, but let us not allow anger to dictate our actions. We must work together to find a solution, not divide ourselves further."*

"But what if we don't see results?" the warrior challenged, defiance evident in his stance.

Mantsopa interjected, her voice fierce yet compassionate. *"What we need is collaboration, not conflict. If we allow our grievances to escalate into violence, we will only bring suffering upon ourselves. We cannot afford that."*

Moshoeshoe sensed a shift in the crowd. Some began to murmur in agreement, the seeds of understanding taking root.

"Let us create a task force," he proposed, *"composed of both Basotho and Matabele members. This group will be responsible for overseeing resource distribution and ensuring that our agreements are upheld. Together, we can find a way forward."*

The suggestion hung in the air, and after a moment of silence, a collective nod of approval spread through the crowd.

"We can hold our leaders accountable," a Matabele elder added, voice strong. *"We will not let fear drive us apart. We will work as one people!"*

With that, the mood began to shift. The forum transformed from a space of tension to one of collaboration. Moshoeshoe felt a surge of hope as ideas flowed freely, and plans took shape.

By the end of the day, they had formed a diverse task force—a blend of voices from both communities, dedicated to fostering unity and cooperation. The spirit of resolve enveloped the gathering, and for the first time in weeks, Moshoeshoe felt the weight on his shoulders lift slightly.

As the forum concluded, Sizwe approached him, a look of gratitude in his eyes. *"You held us together today, Chief. We may not have all the answers yet, but we are moving in the right direction."*

Mantsopa joined them, her smile warm. *"This is just the beginning. We must continue to nurture this dialogue, to ensure that every voice is heard."*

As they made their way home under the setting sun, Moshoeshoe felt a renewed sense of purpose. The road ahead would still be fraught with challenges, but today they had taken a significant step toward healing and understanding.

Yet, deep down, he couldn't shake the feeling that their greatest test was still to come. As they walked in silence, he resolved to remain vigilant, knowing that unity required constant effort and dedication.

Chapter 21: A New Alliance

In the weeks following the forum, the task force became a beacon of hope for both communities. They met regularly, addressing grievances and developing strategies for resource management. Moshoeshoe observed the dynamics between the Basotho and Matabele, a delicate dance of collaboration that slowly began to bear fruit.

The initial meetings were filled with tension, but gradually, as they tackled issues together, trust began to blossom. Shared goals emerged, uniting them in the face of adversity. They developed a plan for a communal irrigation project that would benefit both communities, and discussions of shared farming techniques fostered cooperation.

However, as optimism grew, so did the challenges of the drought. The once-promising clouds that occasionally passed overhead now seemed to dissipate before releasing any rain. The land remained parched, and the specter of desperation loomed larger each day.

One afternoon, while meeting with the task force, Sizwe raised a pressing concern. *"We need to do more. Our people are becoming restless again. Without rain, hope is dwindling. We must find a way to ease their suffering."*

Moshoeshoe nodded, feeling the weight of Sizwe's words. *"You're right. We must not only focus on long-term solutions but also immediate relief. Let's organize a communal gathering to distribute food and supplies."*

Mantsopa added, *"We can ask local farmers to donate what they can spare. It's essential that everyone sees the commitment to supporting one another."*

With renewed determination, the task force mobilized. Flyers were distributed, and a community gathering was organized for the following weekend. As the day approached, excitement mixed with anxiety. They needed to show tangible results to quell the rising tension.

When the day finally arrived, people from both communities gathered at the central meeting place, their expressions a mix of hope and skepticism. Moshoeshoe stood at the forefront, flanked by Mantsopa and Sizwe, ready to address the crowd.

"Thank you for coming today," he began, his voice resonating with warmth. *"We face great challenges, but today we stand united to support one another. Together, we will share resources and reinforce our commitment to this alliance."*

The crowd erupted in murmurs, and as supplies were distributed, a sense of solidarity began to blossom. Individuals from both communities worked side by side, sharing food and stories, their bonds slowly strengthening.

As the gathering progressed, Moshoeshoe felt a swell of pride. They were making strides, and for the first time in weeks, he saw genuine smiles and laughter among the people.

However, the mood shifted when a group of young warriors arrived, their faces hardened with anger. *"What is this?"* one of them shouted. *"We're starving while you waste our resources on these outsiders!"*

Moshoeshoe stepped forward, his heart racing. *"We are all suffering. This gathering is meant to support everyone, to show that we can overcome our struggles together."*

But the warriors were unconvinced. *"You promise unity, yet our lands continue to dry! We need action, not empty words!"*

Sizwe moved closer, his tone measured. *"We understand your frustration. But this gathering is a step toward building trust. We need to show our people that we can work together."*

Mantsopa added, *"Every action counts. If we allow anger to dictate our path, we will only deepen our suffering. Let us work together to find solutions."*

The warriors hesitated, their anger wavering as they absorbed the weight of her words. The crowd watched in silence, the tension palpable.

Moshoeshoe seized the moment. *"We are here today to build a foundation for our future. If we can come together in times of hardship, we can create something strong and lasting. Trust takes time, but it begins with small actions."*

Gradually, the anger in the warriors' eyes began to fade. One of them stepped forward, his voice still defiant but tinged with uncertainty. *"We will give you a chance, but we need to see results."*

"Then let us work," Moshoeshoe replied, a fire igniting within him. *"We will gather resources, strengthen our alliances, and show that together we are stronger. Let's plan a community effort to build a water conservation system, one that benefits us all."*

As the gathering concluded, the mood shifted from hostility to a cautious optimism. The warriors, though still skeptical, began to engage with their fellow community members, and the seeds of understanding were sown.

Later that evening, as Moshoeshoe, Mantsopa, and Sizwe reflected on the day's events, they felt the weight of their journey thus far.

"We've made progress," Sizwe said, a hint of hope in his voice. *"But we must remain vigilant. There are still those who doubt our intentions."*

Mantsopa nodded, her expression serious. "Every step we take is essential. We need to continue nurturing this alliance, even when faced with opposition."

Moshoeshoe felt a surge of determination. *"We cannot allow fear to dictate our actions. If we continue to stand united, we can weather any storm. Our shared history is a testament to our strength."*

As the stars twinkled above Thaba Bosiu, Moshoeshoe held onto the belief that they were moving toward a brighter future. The road ahead would be fraught with challenges, but he knew that together, they could overcome anything.

Chapter 22: Shadows of Dissent

As the days turned into weeks, the efforts of the task force began to yield results. The community's collective action brought about a glimmer of hope. People from both the Basotho and Matabele joined hands to repair water systems and implement conservation practices. Yet, the drought continued to test their resolve.

Despite the progress, whispers of dissent lingered in the shadows. A faction among the young Basotho, disillusioned by the slow pace of change, began to form. They believed that the council was not doing enough to protect their interests, and their frustration grew as the drought persisted.

One evening, as Moshoeshoe and Mantsopa were discussing their plans for the next communal meeting, a messenger arrived, breathless and urgent. *"Chief Moshoeshoe! There is trouble brewing at the riverbank. A group of young warriors is confronting Matabele families there."*

Without hesitation, Moshoeshoe and Mantsopa set out, anxiety clawing at them. As they approached the river, the sounds of raised voices echoed through the air.

When they arrived, they found a heated confrontation. A group of Basotho warriors, led by the same young man from the previous gathering, shouted at a group of Matabele families, accusing them of hoarding resources.

"Step aside!" Moshoeshoe commanded, his voice booming over the commotion. The crowd fell silent, and all eyes turned to him.

"What is happening here?" he demanded, his gaze scanning the tense faces.

"They're stealing our water!" the young warrior yelled, anger flashing in his eyes. *"While we suffer, they take what's ours!"*

Moshoeshoe stepped forward, his heart racing. *"We cannot resolve our issues through conflict. We are all facing the same drought. The water belongs to everyone."*

"But they don't care about us!" another Basotho shouted, frustration evident. *"They think they can take what they want without consequence!"*

Mantsopa interjected, her voice calm yet firm. *"This is not the way forward. If we allow anger and mistrust to guide our actions, we will only deepen our suffering. We must come together, not tear each other apart."*

Sizwe arrived, breathless, and stood beside Moshoeshoe. *"Let us resolve this together. We must create a system for water distribution that is fair and transparent."*

The young warrior hesitated, uncertainty flickering across his face. *"And how can we trust that they will share? We have been left wanting for too long!"*

"We will oversee the process together," Sizwe assured him. *"Both communities will have representatives, ensuring that fairness prevails."*

After a tense silence, the warrior nodded, still reluctant but willing to consider the proposal.

"Let us hold a meeting to establish these guidelines," Moshoeshoe proposed, his tone resolute. *"If we work together, we can build a framework that supports everyone's needs."*

Gradually, the tension in the air began to dissipate. Moshoeshoe felt a sense of relief wash over him. While mistrust lingered, they had a chance to forge a path forward.

As they left the riverbank, Mantsopa turned to Moshoeshoe, her expression serious. *"This unrest is a sign that we need to act decisively. If we don't address these concerns, we risk losing the progress we've made."*

"I know," he replied, concern etched on his face. *"But we must also remain patient. Unity is a delicate balance, and we must tread carefully."*

In the following days, Moshoeshoe worked tirelessly to organize the meeting. He reached out to both communities, encouraging them to participate and voice their concerns. The atmosphere was charged with tension as the date approached.

On the day of the meeting, a palpable sense of unease hung in the air. The council chamber was filled with people, their expressions a mix of hope and skepticism. Moshoeshoe stood at the forefront, flanked by Mantsopa and Sizwe.

"Thank you all for coming," he began, his voice steady. *"Today, we gather not just to address our challenges, but to reaffirm our commitment to one another. The drought affects us all, and we must ensure that resources are shared equitably."*

As he spoke, he could see some warriors exchanging glances, their skepticism evident.

"I urge you to share your concerns openly," he continued, gesturing toward the assembled crowd. *"Let us find common ground and build a plan that supports everyone."*

The first speaker, an elder from the Matabele community, stepped forward. *"We are all suffering, and we must work together to manage our resources. But trust must be rebuilt. We need to ensure transparency in our actions."*

A young Basotho warrior rose to speak, his expression defiant. *"How can we trust you when we see our families suffer? We need to see real action, not just words!"*

The room buzzed with tension as voices rose in agreement. Moshoeshoe felt the weight of their anger pressing down on him. *"I understand your pain,"* he said, his voice steady. *"We are all facing this drought together. But if we let anger guide our actions, we will lose everything we have worked for."*

The dialogue continued, and while some voices sought to escalate the conflict, others urged for unity. Gradually, ideas emerged for a fair water distribution system, and the crowd began to engage more constructively.

As the meeting progressed, Moshoeshoe felt a sense of cautious optimism. They were navigating through the storm of discontent, slowly finding their way toward solutions.

But as the gathering came to a close, he couldn't shake the feeling that the shadows of dissent were still lurking, waiting for an opportunity to strike.

In the days that followed, Moshoeshoe remained vigilant, knowing that the road ahead would require continued effort, patience, and above all, unity.

Chapter 23: The Breaking Point

As the weeks passed, the fragile alliance between the Basotho and Matabele hung in a delicate balance. The drought continued to ravage the land, and despite their efforts to cooperate, discontent simmered just beneath the surface. The task force worked diligently to establish the water distribution system, but progress was slow and fraught with setbacks.

One evening, Moshoeshoe received word of a serious incident at the communal water point. He gathered Mantsopa and Sizwe and rushed to the scene, his heart racing.

When they arrived, chaos greeted them. A crowd of Basotho warriors had gathered, their faces filled with anger and frustration. At the center of the commotion stood a group of Matabele families, fearful and defensive.

"What is happening?" Moshoeshoe demanded, stepping into the fray.

"They're taking more than their share!" a young Basotho shouted, pointing an accusatory finger at the Matabele. *"While our families starve, they hoard the water!"*

Moshoeshoe felt his stomach drop. *"We must not resort to violence. Everyone here is suffering! Let us resolve this calmly."*

But the tension had reached a breaking point. Voices clashed, and anger ignited like wildfire. A warrior pushed forward, shouting, *"We need to take control! If they won't share, we will take what is ours!"*

Mantsopa stepped in, her voice ringing with authority. *"This is not the way! If we allow anger to dictate our actions, we will tear our communities apart."*

The crowd wavered between aggression and hesitation, caught in the storm of their emotions. Sizwe tried to mediate, stepping closer to the warriors. *"We must remember why we came together. This conflict will only lead to more suffering for everyone. We need a solution, not a fight."*

Just as it seemed the situation might deescalate, a sudden shout pierced the air. A young Matabele, pushed to the brink by fear, threw a stone toward the warriors. It missed its mark but shattered the fragile calm.

In an instant, the crowd erupted into chaos. Warriors charged, shouting and clashing with one another. Moshoeshoe felt the ground shake beneath him, his heart pounding. He rushed forward, desperate to intervene.

"Stop!" he bellowed, his voice echoing over the chaos. *"This is not the way! We cannot allow anger to destroy what we have built together!"*

But his words were drowned out by the roar of the crowd. Fists flew, and the atmosphere turned hostile. Moshoeshoe fought through the throng, pulling warriors apart, trying to restore some semblance of order.

Mantsopa joined him, her determination unwavering. *"We must stop this! We are all suffering!"*

With great effort, they managed to separate the warring factions, but the damage had been done. The sense of unity they had worked so hard to build had crumbled, and the fear of conflict loomed larger than ever.

Finally, as the dust began to settle, Moshoeshoe stood before the crowd, breathing heavily, anger and frustration evident in his eyes. *"Look at what we have become! We are letting our suffering blind us to the truth—we are stronger together, not divided by conflict!"*

The crowd, though still restless, began to quiet. Moshoeshoe saw the pain in their eyes, the realization that this path would lead to their mutual destruction.

"We must hold another forum," he continued, his voice steady. *"A place where we can openly discuss our fears and grievances. Only by confronting our issues can we find a way forward."*

Sizwe stepped forward, looking around at the weary faces. *"We need to set aside our anger and work together. If we allow mistrust to divide us, we will lose everything we've fought for."*

After a long pause, a young woman from the Basotho stepped forward, her voice trembling but resolute. *"I want to believe in this unity. But we need to see real action. We cannot survive on promises alone."*

Moshoeshoe nodded, feeling the weight of her words. *"Then let us commit to action. We will gather again, and we will establish concrete plans to ensure fairness in our resource distribution. We will take immediate steps to address your concerns."*

As the crowd began to disperse, Moshoeshoe felt a mixture of relief and apprehension. The path ahead was fraught with challenges, but he knew that they had to confront their differences head-on.

In the days leading up to the next forum, Moshoeshoe worked tirelessly with Mantsopa and Sizwe to prepare. They gathered feedback from both communities, determined to create a comprehensive plan that would address the root causes of their discontent.

On the day of the forum, the atmosphere was thick with tension. As people filled the gathering place, Moshoeshoe stood at the forefront, flanked by Mantsopa and Sizwe. He could sense the unease among the crowd, the lingering distrust palpable.

"Thank you for coming," he began, his voice resonating with authority. *"Today, we face a critical moment. We must confront the challenges that divide us and forge a path toward unity."*

The first speaker, a weary Matabele elder, stepped forward. *"We have suffered too long in silence. It is time for transparency. We must share what we have, not just in words but in action."*

A young Basotho warrior followed, his expression fierce. *"We need to see results! Promises mean nothing when our families are hungry."*

Moshoeshoe listened intently, his heart heavy with the weight of their grievances. *"We are here to build trust, and that begins with accountability. Together, we will outline a plan that ensures fair resource distribution and immediate support for those in need."*

As the discussions unfolded, Moshoeshoe felt the atmosphere begin to shift. The warriors, while still skeptical, engaged in dialogue, expressing their fears and frustrations. Slowly, a sense of shared purpose began to emerge.

By the end of the forum, they had established a plan—a series of actions aimed at ensuring fairness and transparency. Moshoeshoe felt a flicker of hope, but he knew that the road ahead would be fraught with challenges.

As the gathering concluded, Moshoeshoe turned to Mantsopa and Sizwe, their expressions resolute. *"This is just the beginning. We must remain vigilant and continue to foster this alliance."*

But deep down, he felt the shadows of dissent lurking, ready to strike again if they did not navigate their path with care. The struggle for unity was far from over, and the greatest tests were yet to come.

Chapter 24: The Gathering Storm

The days following the forum were marked by a fragile sense of hope. Moshoeshoe, Mantsopa, and Sizwe worked tirelessly to implement the new plan. Resources were mobilized, and the task force organized regular meetings to ensure transparency in the distribution process. For a moment, it seemed as if the storm clouds of dissent had parted, allowing sunlight to break through.

However, beneath the surface, unease simmered. The drought showed no signs of abating, and desperation crept into the hearts of many. Rumors began to circulate, whispers of betrayal and mistrust that threatened to undermine their fragile alliance.

One evening, Moshoeshoe convened a meeting with Mantsopa and Sizwe. *"We need to address the rumors,"* he said, concern etched on his face. *"If we do not confront this, it could tear apart everything we've built."*

Mantsopa nodded. *"The longer we let uncertainty fester, the stronger the shadows will grow. We must reaffirm our commitment to transparency and community."*

Sizwe added, *"Perhaps we should hold a gathering to openly discuss these concerns. We need to create a safe space for everyone to voice their fears."*

With a sense of urgency, they organized a meeting for the following week, hoping to quell the rising tide of discontent. As the day approached, tension hung in the air like a thick fog.

On the day of the gathering, people filled the meeting place, their expressions a mix of hope and apprehension. Moshoeshoe stood before them, flanked by Mantsopa and Sizwe, ready to address the crowd.

"Thank you for coming," he began, his voice steady but filled with emotion. *"Today, we gather not just to discuss our challenges, but to reaffirm our unity. We must confront the fears that divide us, and work together to build a better future."*

The crowd murmured, a mix of skepticism and curiosity. Moshoeshoe could feel the weight of their gazes, each person searching for reassurance.

As the first speaker—a young woman from the Matabele community—stepped forward, she addressed the crowd with a tremor in her voice. *"We are all suffering. We've heard rumors that some of our leaders are hoarding resources for their own families while the rest of us starve. How can we trust that this alliance will truly benefit us?"*

The room fell silent, the tension palpable. Moshoeshoe felt his heart race. *"I understand your concerns, and I assure you that transparency is our priority. We must hold each other accountable to build trust."*

A young Basotho warrior interjected, anger flaring in his eyes. *"And what if that trust is broken? We've seen leaders fail us before. What guarantees do we have that this time will be different?"*

Moshoeshoe took a deep breath, trying to quell the rising tide of emotion. *"We can only move forward through open dialogue. If there are specific grievances, let us address them. We are all in this together."*

As the meeting progressed, voices rose and fell like the waves of the ocean. Concerns were voiced, accusations hurled, but amid the turmoil, moments of understanding began to emerge. The desire for cooperation and shared survival overshadowed the fear that had once threatened to tear them apart.

Mantsopa stepped forward, her voice cutting through the chaos. *"We must remember why we are here. We face a common enemy—the drought that seeks to destroy us all. If we allow our distrust to guide us, we will fall victim to it."*

The crowd began to quiet, their attention turning to her. *"Let us not forget that our strength lies in our unity. Together, we can weather this storm."*

As the gathering continued, they began to outline concrete steps for accountability. They formed smaller committees to oversee resource distribution, ensuring that every voice would be heard.

Yet, even as they made progress, Moshoeshoe felt a lingering unease. The shadows of dissent had not completely faded; he could sense that the fears were still alive, waiting for an opportunity to resurface.

In the days that followed, Moshoeshoe, Mantsopa, and Sizwe continued their work, pushing to implement the new measures. They visited families, listened to concerns, and provided updates on their efforts. For a moment, it felt as though hope was beginning to take root.

But just as they began to gain traction, disaster struck. News arrived of a raid by a group of Matabele warriors on a Basotho settlement, sparked by accusations that the Basotho were hoarding water. The anger that had been simmering erupted into violence, and panic swept through both communities.

Moshoeshoe gathered Mantsopa and Sizwe, determination fueling his every word. "We cannot let this spiral out of control. We must act quickly to prevent further bloodshed."

They set out to intervene, urgency driving them forward. When they reached the settlement, the scene was chaotic. Families were fleeing, and the sounds of conflict echoed in the air. Moshoeshoe felt his heart pound in his chest as he fought to maintain his composure.

"*Stop!*" he shouted, stepping into the fray, his presence commanding attention. "*This is not the way! We cannot allow anger to destroy our communities!*"

As he spoke, Mantsopa and Sizwe moved to calm the warriors, trying to break through the cloud of rage. "*We need to listen to one another,*" Mantsopa urged, her voice firm but compassionate. "*If we don't, we risk losing everything we've fought for.*"

Gradually, the warriors began to lower their weapons, confusion overtaking their anger. The violence began to subside as Moshoeshoe worked to restore order, his heart heavy with the knowledge that the divisions between them had deepened once again.

In the aftermath, as night fell and the fires dimmed, Moshoeshoe gathered the leaders from both communities. "*We are at a breaking point,*" he said, his voice grave. "*If we do not come together now, we risk losing not only our alliance but our very lives. We must unite against the true enemy—the drought and the suffering it brings.*"

The leaders nodded, the weight of the moment settling heavily upon them. They knew that the road ahead would be difficult, but they also understood that unity was their only path forward.

As Moshoeshoe looked into the eyes of his people, he felt a surge of determination. He would not let despair extinguish their hope. Together, they could rise from the ashes of conflict and forge a future that would honor their shared struggle.

But as he prepared to face the challenges ahead, he couldn't shake the feeling that the storm was far from over.

Chapter 25: The Call to Unity

The aftermath of the raid left both communities shaken, the scars of violence etched deep in their memories. Tensions ran high as families mourned lost livestock and bruised pride. Moshoeshoe knew that the time for action was now, and he needed to bring both sides together to heal the wounds that had been opened.

In the days following the incident, Moshoeshoe called for an emergency gathering at Thaba Bosiu, the sacred mountain that held deep significance for the Basotho. It was a place of refuge, a symbol of strength and resilience. He hoped that standing together on this ground would remind them of their shared heritage and purpose.

As the day of the gathering arrived, the air was thick with anticipation. Warriors from both communities stood at the foot of the mountain, their expressions a mixture of defiance and uncertainty. Mantsopa and Sizwe stood beside Moshoeshoe, ready to address the crowd.

"Today, we come together not as Basotho and Matabele," Moshoeshoe began, his voice resonating against the backdrop of the mountain. *"We gather as brothers and sisters, united in our struggle against the forces that seek to tear us apart."*

A murmur swept through the crowd, and Moshoeshoe continued, *"The drought is our common enemy, and it thrives on our discord. We cannot afford to let anger and mistrust dictate our actions. Our survival depends on our ability to work together."*

A young Basotho warrior stepped forward, his tone challenging. *"How can we trust the Matabele after what happened? Lives were lost, and resources were taken! What guarantees do we have that this alliance will protect us?"*

Moshoeshoe felt the weight of his words, but he pressed on. *"Trust is earned, and it must be built on action. We need to create a joint council with equal representation from both communities. Together, we can oversee resource distribution and ensure that everyone's needs are met."*

The young warrior hesitated, uncertainty flickering in his eyes. *"And if the council fails us?"*

"Then we will hold each other accountable," Mantsopa interjected, her voice strong. *"We must agree to be transparent and open about our actions. This is our chance to redefine our relationship."*

Another voice rose from the crowd, this time from a Matabele elder. *"We have all suffered. If we allow this moment to slip away, we will only perpetuate the cycle of violence. We must embrace this opportunity for unity."*

Gradually, the crowd began to engage, exchanging ideas and expressing their fears. The discussions evolved into a constructive dialogue, a blend of passion and vulnerability that began to bridge the divide.

As the sun dipped lower in the sky, casting a golden glow over the mountain, Moshoeshoe felt a surge of hope. *"Let us make a pact today,"* he proposed. *"A promise to work together, to share resources, and to protect one another. Our future depends on our unity."*

With the crowd's support, they formalized the creation of the joint council, a symbol of their commitment to cooperation. They outlined specific steps for resource management, including equitable access to water and food supplies.

As the gathering came to a close, a sense of purpose enveloped them. They had taken a significant step toward healing the rift between their communities, but Moshoeshoe knew that the journey ahead would not be easy.

In the weeks that followed, the joint council convened regularly, working to implement the agreed-upon measures. They conducted community surveys, addressing concerns and fostering dialogue. For the first time in a long while, there was a palpable sense of collaboration, with members from both communities contributing their ideas.

However, as they celebrated small victories, the drought continued to cast a long shadow over their efforts. Water sources dwindled, and tensions remained just below the surface, threatening to resurface at any moment.

One afternoon, as Moshoeshoe visited a well, he overheard a heated discussion among a group of young Basotho. They were frustrated, their voices rising in anger.

"*This council is a joke!*" one of them exclaimed. "*We're still starving while they sit in their meetings, making empty promises!*"

Moshoeshoe approached cautiously, raising his hand to signal for calm. "*What troubles you?*"

"*While we toil for scraps, the Matabele have more than enough!*" another warrior shouted. "*This alliance isn't working for us. We need to take matters into our own hands!*"

Moshoeshoe felt a familiar sense of urgency. "*Violence will not solve our problems. It will only lead to more suffering. We must continue to work together and communicate our needs to the council.*"

"*But what if they ignore us?*" the first warrior challenged.

"*Then we must hold them accountable,*" Moshoeshoe replied firmly. "*We can't allow frustration to dictate our actions. Instead, we must channel that energy into constructive dialogue.*"

Though their expressions were still filled with doubt, some of the warriors nodded, absorbing his words. Moshoeshoe felt a glimmer of hope that they might find a way through their frustration.

As the days turned into weeks, the joint council made progress in addressing the immediate needs of both communities. They organized communal food distributions and established a system for sharing water resources. Slowly but surely, trust began to rebuild.

But the drought raged on, relentless and unforgiving. The specter of despair loomed over them, a constant reminder of the stakes at hand.

One evening, as Moshoeshoe sat beneath the stars, he contemplated the weight of leadership. The challenges were immense, but the resilience of his people inspired him. He knew that he had to find a way to sustain their hope, even in the darkest of times.

In that moment of reflection, he made a silent vow—to lead with integrity, to foster unity, and to fight for a future where all could thrive together.

But as he looked toward the horizon, he felt the winds of change stirring. The storm was not yet over, and he could sense that greater challenges lay ahead.

Chapter 26: The Test of Unity

As the festival concluded, a sense of hope lingered in the air, but the reality of their struggles was never far behind. The rains had finally come, bringing relief to the parched earth, but with them came new challenges. Floodwaters swelled in the rivers, threatening both Basotho and Matabele settlements.

One evening, Moshoeshoe received urgent news from the council: the rising waters had breached the banks of the river, endangering homes and livelihoods. He gathered Mantsopa and Sizwe, their faces grim as they prepared to address the impending crisis.

"We must act quickly," Moshoeshoe said, urgency in his voice. *"We need to organize evacuation efforts and provide support for those in danger."*

The three leaders moved swiftly, rallying volunteers from both communities. As night fell, they formed teams to assess the damage and assist families in need. Moshoeshoe felt the weight of leadership heavy upon him, aware that this crisis could either strengthen their alliance or unravel it entirely.

As they arrived at the riverbank, chaos reigned. People were scrambling to gather their belongings, fear etched on their faces. The sound of rushing water echoed in the background, a stark reminder of the threat they faced.

"Stay calm!" Moshoeshoe shouted as he moved through the crowd. *"We are here to help. Gather your families and follow our lead!"*

Mantsopa worked alongside him, comforting those in distress and helping them prioritize what to take. Sizwe coordinated the volunteers, directing them to assist families with evacuating. Together, they formed a chain, guiding people away from the rising waters.

But as the night wore on, tensions flared. A group of young Basotho grew restless, frustrated by what they perceived as a lack of urgency from their Matabele neighbors. *"They're taking too long!"* one of them shouted, pointing angrily. *"We need to get to safety!"*

"Hold on!" a Matabele youth retorted. *"We're doing our best! Everyone is in danger here!"*

Moshoeshoe sensed the shift in mood, the undercurrents of distrust threatening to surface. *"Listen to me!"* he called out, his voice cutting through the din. *"This is not the time for division! We must work together to ensure everyone's safety!"*

The crowd paused, caught between their emotions and the urgency of the situation. Mantsopa stepped forward, her tone firm yet soothing. *"This is our moment to prove that we can rise above our fears and work together. We cannot let anger cloud our judgment."*

Gradually, their words began to resonate. The warriors and families shifted their focus back to the task at hand. Moshoeshoe felt a flicker of hope, but he knew that the night was far from over.

As they continued their efforts, Moshoeshoe noticed a family stranded near the river's edge, their home swept away by the flood. He rushed over, his heart racing. *"We need to get them to safety!"* he called out.

Without hesitation, several volunteers joined him, forming a human chain to reach the family. The waters surged dangerously close, but they pressed on, determination fueling their actions. With a collective effort, they managed to pull the family to safety, cheers erupting from those gathered.

But just as they celebrated this small victory, a loud crack echoed in the distance. A tree, weakened by the flood, fell with a thunderous crash, narrowly missing a group of evacuees. Panic surged through the crowd as chaos erupted once more.

"Stay calm! Move to higher ground!" Moshoeshoe shouted, his voice ringing out amid the turmoil. He fought to maintain order, rallying the volunteers to guide everyone to safety.

In the midst of the chaos, he caught sight of the young Basotho who had previously voiced their frustration. The warrior stood frozen, fear and doubt etched on his face. Moshoeshoe approached him, placing a hand on his shoulder.

"*Now is the time to lead,*" he urged. "*Help us guide your people. Show them that we can overcome this together.*"

The young man hesitated, then nodded, determination replacing his fear. He turned to his fellow warriors, rallying them to assist in the evacuation. Slowly, the crowd began to stabilize, moving as a unified force toward higher ground.

As dawn broke, the waters finally receded, revealing the devastation left in their wake. Families gathered at a designated safe area, their faces weary but relieved. Moshoeshoe and the council set up a temporary shelter, providing food and comfort to those in need.

Exhausted yet resolute, Moshoeshoe addressed the crowd once more. "*We have faced the storm together, and though we have suffered loss, we have proven that our unity can withstand even the greatest challenges.*"

A murmur of agreement swept through the crowd, and for the first time since the floods began, hope flickered in their eyes. Mantsopa stepped forward, her voice strong. "*Let us honor those we have lost by rebuilding together. We will not let this disaster define us.*"

As the community began to heal, Moshoeshoe knew that the road ahead would be long. They would have to confront the aftermath of the floods, rebuilding homes and restoring livelihoods. But they had also forged a deeper bond—a shared understanding that their survival depended on their commitment to one another.

In the months that followed, they worked tirelessly to rebuild, each day strengthening the ties between their communities. The experience had transformed them, weaving a new narrative of resilience and solidarity.

As Moshoeshoe stood on Thaba Bosiu, watching the sunrise over the land they had fought so hard to protect, he felt a deep sense of gratitude. The path to unity was fraught with challenges, but together, they had proven that they could weather any storm.

Chapter 27: Rebuilding Hope

As the sun rose over the ravaged landscape, the remnants of the flood lay scattered across the valley. The once-familiar homes of the Basotho and Matabele were now mere shadows of what they had been, the waters having swept away not only structures but also a sense of normalcy.

Yet amid the devastation, a spirit of resilience ignited within the communities. The joint council convened, determined to address the immediate needs of those affected and to forge a path toward recovery.

"*Today, we must focus on rebuilding,*" Moshoeshoe announced at the council meeting, his voice steady but laced with urgency. "*We will need to pool our resources and ensure that no one is left behind. Our survival depends on our unity.*"

Mantsopa nodded, her gaze sweeping across the gathered leaders. "*We must also address the emotional toll this disaster has taken. People will need support to cope with their loss. We can organize community gatherings to facilitate healing and discussion.*"

Sizwe spoke up, "*And we must restore essential services—clean water, food supplies, and shelter. We can work with neighboring tribes to source additional resources.*"

The council members nodded in agreement, their determination palpable. They divided into teams, each taking responsibility for specific areas: resource management, community support, and infrastructure rebuilding.

As they dispersed, Moshoeshoe felt a renewed sense of purpose. He visited the affected families, offering words of comfort and assurance. "*We will rebuild together. This community has endured hardships before, and we will rise again.*"

In the days that followed, the spirit of cooperation flourished. Volunteers from both communities came together to clear debris and start the rebuilding process. The sound of laughter and shared stories filled the air, a testament to their shared commitment to overcome adversity.

One afternoon, as they worked side by side, Moshoeshoe noticed the young Basotho warrior who had stepped up during the flood crisis. He was engaged in conversation with a Matabele woman, their laughter mingling with the sounds of construction.

Moshoeshoe approached, a smile breaking across his face. "*It's good to see you both working together,*" he said, his heart warmed by the sight of unity blossoming amid the rubble.

The young warrior turned, his expression bright. "*We've learned that we're stronger together. We're sharing skills and ideas, building not just homes but relationships.*"

Mantsopa joined them, her eyes shining with pride. "*This is the essence of our alliance. We are not just rebuilding structures; we are rebuilding trust and community.*"

As the weeks turned into months, the landscape transformed. New homes began to rise from the ashes, their walls adorned with symbols of both cultures—a fusion of Matabele and Basotho traditions that celebrated their unity.

But as progress was made, old fears and tensions lingered just beneath the surface. Whispers of dissent resurfaced, fueled by those who still felt marginalized or unheard. Some voiced concerns that resources were not being distributed fairly, while others questioned the effectiveness of the joint council.

One evening, as the sun set behind the mountains, Moshoeshoe and Mantsopa convened a community meeting to address these growing concerns. The atmosphere was charged, with community members expressing their frustrations openly.

"*Why should we trust that this council will prioritize our needs?*" a Matabele elder questioned, his tone pointed. "*We have been here before, and our voices have gone unheard.*"

Moshoeshoe took a deep breath, recognizing the gravity of the moment. "*I understand your concerns, and I acknowledge the pain that many of you feel. But we are here to listen, to learn, and to grow together. We cannot move forward unless we confront these issues openly.*"

Mantsopa stepped forward, her voice steady. *"Let us create a platform where everyone can voice their concerns. Transparency is key. We need to ensure that every voice matters."*

As the discussion unfolded, people began to share their stories, their fears, and their hopes. Some felt that their needs were overlooked, while others expressed gratitude for the progress made thus far. The conversation grew more constructive as they brainstormed solutions together.

By the end of the meeting, the community had proposed a series of actionable steps. They would establish a feedback system to track resource distribution, hold regular forums to address concerns, and create committees focused on inclusivity.

Moshoeshoe felt a sense of relief as the meeting concluded. They had turned a moment of tension into an opportunity for growth, reinforcing the foundations of their alliance.

In the weeks that followed, they implemented the proposed changes, fostering a culture of transparency and collaboration. Gradually, trust began to rebuild, and a newfound sense of community emerged.

As Moshoeshoe surveyed the progress from the top of Thaba Bosiu, he marveled at how far they had come. The landscape was dotted with new homes, and the laughter of children echoed through the valley. They had faced trials that could have torn them apart but instead had woven them closer together.

But as he stood there, a sense of foreboding lingered in his heart. He knew that while they had made significant strides, the road ahead would still be fraught with challenges. The world outside their alliance was unpredictable, and they would need to remain vigilant.

As night fell, Moshoeshoe made a silent vow to continue leading with integrity and compassion. He would ensure that the lessons learned from their struggles would guide them as they navigated the complexities of their alliance.

Together, they would face whatever storms lay ahead, united in their commitment to forge a future that honored their shared humanity.

Chapter 28: Shadows of Doubt

As the community continued to rebuild, the seasons changed, and the resilience of the Basotho and Matabele alliance began to bear fruit. New crops sprouted in the fields, and the laughter of children filled the air once more. Yet, beneath the surface, unease simmered.

Rumors of external threats began to circulate. Some neighboring tribes, feeling threatened by the unity displayed between the Basotho and Matabele, whispered of potential conflict. Moshoeshoe sensed the growing tension, and the council convened to address these concerns.

"Unity has made us stronger, but it has also drawn the attention of those who would seek to divide us," Moshoeshoe warned the council, his voice serious. *"We must be prepared for any challenges that may arise."*

Sizwe, always pragmatic, nodded in agreement. *"We need to strengthen our defenses and maintain open lines of communication. We should organize joint patrols to keep an eye on the borders."*

Mantsopa raised her hand. *"But we must also remember that fear can lead to rash decisions. We cannot let paranoia dictate our actions. Instead, let's hold a gathering to reassure our communities and reaffirm our commitment to peace."*

As the council agreed to Mantsopa's proposal, Moshoeshoe felt a weight lift from his shoulders. They had weathered storms together before, and this was yet another opportunity to strengthen their bond.

The day of the gathering arrived, and the atmosphere was charged with anticipation. Community members from both sides gathered at Thaba Bosiu, their faces reflecting a mix of hope and apprehension.

Moshoeshoe stood before them, flanked by Mantsopa and Sizwe. *"Today, we come together not just to celebrate our unity, but to prepare ourselves for the challenges that lie ahead. We must remain vigilant but not let fear dictate our actions."*

The crowd listened intently as Mantsopa continued, *"We have built something beautiful here—a community that thrives on trust and collaboration. We will not allow outside forces to disrupt what we have achieved."*

After their speeches, community members broke into smaller groups, discussing ways to enhance their security while promoting peace. Moshoeshoe moved among them, listening to their ideas and concerns, feeling the pulse of the alliance.

But as night fell, a sense of foreboding lingered. Moshoeshoe gathered his closest advisors to discuss a troubling report he had received: a neighboring tribe had begun to mobilize, rumored to be planning an incursion into their territory.

"We cannot ignore this," Sizwe said, his brow furrowed. *"We need to send scouts to gather more information. We must know their intentions before we act."*

Mantsopa spoke up, her voice steady. *"But we must tread carefully. Any aggressive move could provoke conflict. We should explore the possibility of diplomacy first."*

Moshoeshoe weighed their words carefully. *"Let us send scouts to assess the situation, but we should also reach out to their leaders. We cannot let misunderstanding escalate into violence."*

The following days were tense. Scouts reported back, confirming the mobilization of the neighboring tribe. Moshoeshoe and the council prepared for the worst while hoping for a peaceful resolution.

A few days later, a delegation from the neighboring tribe arrived at Thaba Bosiu, led by a chief known for his cunning. The air crackled with tension as the two sides met, each wary of the other's intentions.

"Why do you come to our lands?" Moshoeshoe asked, his voice firm yet measured.

The chief regarded him with a calculating gaze. *"We come seeking answers. We have watched your alliance grow stronger, and we cannot ignore it. Is it true you intend to claim more territory?"*

Moshoeshoe shook his head. *"Our aim is not to claim what is not ours but to protect our communities from external threats. We seek peace and mutual respect."*

The chief's expression softened slightly, but suspicion lingered. "*You speak of peace, yet your actions tell another story. We have heard whispers of your growing power. What assurances can you provide that you do not seek to dominate?*"

Mantsopa interjected, her voice unwavering. "*We stand for cooperation, not conquest. Our unity is rooted in mutual benefit. Together, we can face challenges without resorting to violence.*"

A tense silence fell over the gathering. The chief considered their words carefully, the weight of history pressing upon them. After a long pause, he spoke, "*Very well. Let us set aside our swords for now. But know this: if we feel threatened, we will defend ourselves.*"

Moshoeshoe nodded, grateful for the opportunity to build a bridge rather than a barrier. "*Let us work toward a future where we can coexist peacefully. Our shared challenges are greater than any rivalry.*"

As the delegation departed, Moshoeshoe felt a mix of relief and apprehension. They had taken a step toward diplomacy, but the shadows of doubt still loomed large.

In the days that followed, Moshoeshoe and the council continued to monitor the situation, maintaining open channels of communication with the neighboring tribe. They organized joint community events to foster goodwill, hoping to dispel any lingering fears.

But as tensions eased, Moshoeshoe could not shake the feeling that the peace was fragile. He knew that unity required constant nurturing, and they would need to remain vigilant against both external threats and internal divisions.

As he looked out over the valley from Thaba Bosiu, he felt the weight of leadership pressing down on him. He understood that true strength lay not just in their defenses, but in their ability to cultivate trust and resilience within their communities.

With Mantsopa by his side, he silently vowed to protect the fragile bonds they had forged, knowing that the path to unity was a continuous journey—one that would require unwavering commitment and courage in the face of adversity.

Chapter 29: Whispers of War

As weeks turned into months, the tension in the region fluctuated like the changing seasons. The initial warmth of diplomacy with the neighboring tribe had faded, replaced by an undercurrent of mistrust. While community events had fostered some goodwill, rumors of hostility persisted, unsettling the alliance.

One evening, as Moshoeshoe sat with Mantsopa and Sizwe in the council chamber, an urgent report arrived from the scouts. *"The neighboring tribe is fortifying their borders,"* the messenger said, his face drawn. *"They appear to be preparing for conflict."*

Moshoeshoe's heart sank. *"We offered them peace, and yet they respond with weapons?"* He felt a deep frustration brewing. *"We need to confront this head-on before it escalates."*

Mantsopa, always the voice of reason, countered, *"Rushing into conflict will only reinforce their fears. We should send a message of peace, reaffirming our commitment to dialogue."*

Sizwe nodded, but concern lingered in his eyes. *"And if they ignore our overtures? We can't be naive. We must also prepare for the worst."*

They decided to send a delegation to the neighboring tribe once more, hoping to clarify their intentions and prevent any misunderstandings. Moshoeshoe chose Sizwe to lead the delegation, knowing his diplomatic skills and experience would be crucial.

As the delegation prepared to leave, tension hung in the air. Community members gathered, expressing their anxieties and fears. *"What if they see this as a sign of weakness?"* one warrior asked. *"We must be ready to defend ourselves."*

"We will be prepared," Moshoeshoe reassured them. *"But let us first seek peace. We cannot let fear dictate our actions."*

Sizwe led the delegation to the neighboring tribe's encampment, where a heavy atmosphere enveloped the meeting. The chief met them with a guarded expression, flanked by his warriors, their eyes scanning the Basotho with suspicion.

"Why do you come again?" the chief asked, his tone cool. *"You think words will change our minds?"*

Sizwe stepped forward, his voice steady. *"We come in peace. We seek to clarify our intentions and ensure that misunderstandings do not lead to conflict. Our alliance is built on cooperation, not aggression."*

The chief's gaze hardened. *"You speak of peace, yet your presence is a reminder of your growing power. How can we trust that you do not harbor ambitions of conquest?"*

"We have no desire to dominate," Sizwe replied, maintaining eye contact. *"Our strength lies in our unity, and we believe that together we can face the challenges of this land without resorting to violence."*

A tense silence settled over the gathering, and Sizwe could see the flicker of doubt in the chief's eyes. After a moment, the chief replied, "We will consider your words. But know this: any sign of weakness from your alliance will be seen as an invitation for conflict."

As Sizwe returned to his community, he felt the weight of uncertainty pressing down. Moshoeshoe and Mantsopa awaited him, their expressions anxious.

"What did they say?" Moshoeshoe asked.

"They listened, but the chief remains skeptical," Sizwe admitted. *"We must show them that we are committed to peace, but I fear their readiness for war may overshadow our efforts."*

Over the following weeks, the council organized training sessions for warriors from both communities, blending their skills and strategies to prepare for potential conflict. The workshops were marked by a mix of camaraderie and tension as they shared techniques and built trust.

Yet, despite their preparations, Moshoeshoe could not shake the feeling of impending doom. He walked through the community, observing the growing anxiety in the eyes of his people. He understood that a single misstep could plunge them into chaos.

One night, as Moshoeshoe stood on Thaba Bosiu, the night sky glittered above him. But beneath that beauty, darkness loomed. He felt the need for a bold gesture to reassure his people and demonstrate their commitment to peace.

The following day, he announced a grand gathering—an event that would invite leaders from neighboring tribes to share food, stories, and songs. "*We will show them that we are a people of peace,*" he declared, his voice resolute. "*Let our actions speak louder than any words.*"

The community rallied around the idea, pouring their energy into preparations. They set up an open space, decorated with vibrant banners representing both cultures, and prepared a feast that would showcase their shared heritage.

On the day of the gathering, the atmosphere was electric. Leaders from various tribes arrived, some skeptical, others curious. Moshoeshoe welcomed them with open arms, offering them food and a place at their table.

As they sat together, sharing stories and laughter, Moshoeshoe felt a flicker of hope. Perhaps this gesture could bridge the divide, reminding everyone of the strength found in unity.

But as the sun set and the festivities reached their peak, a commotion erupted at the edge of the gathering. A group of young warriors from the neighboring tribe had clashed with some of Moshoeshoe's men, their voices raised in anger.

Moshoeshoe rushed to the scene, his heart racing. "*What is happening?*" he demanded, trying to maintain control.

"*They insulted us!*" one of his warriors shouted, fists clenched. "*They think we are weak for celebrating with them!*"

The neighboring chief stepped forward, his eyes narrowing. "*This is not what we agreed upon. Your warriors disrespect our presence!*"

Realizing the potential for conflict spiraling out of control, Moshoeshoe raised his hands. "*Stop! This gathering is meant to promote peace, not violence. We cannot allow a misunderstanding to escalate into war.*"

Silence fell over the crowd as they watched, tension palpable. Moshoeshoe turned to the young warriors, his voice calm yet firm. "*We are stronger together. We cannot let pride dictate our actions.*"

Gradually, the anger in the eyes of the warriors softened, and one of the Matabele stepped forward. "*We are all here for the same reason—to find common ground. Let us not forget that.*"

Moshoeshoe took a deep breath, feeling the weight of the moment. "*Tonight, we celebrate our shared humanity. Let us come together as allies, not enemies. We are stronger united.*"

Slowly, the tension began to dissolve, and the warriors reluctantly lowered their fists. The chief nodded, and the atmosphere shifted as they resumed the festivities, albeit with a lingering caution.

As night fell, Moshoeshoe felt the gravity of what had almost transpired. They had narrowly avoided a conflict, but the fragility of their alliance remained evident. He knew that while they had taken steps toward peace, the shadows of doubt still loomed large.

As the stars twinkled above, Moshoeshoe vowed to continue his efforts, forging a path toward unity and understanding. He understood that true strength lay not just in their ability to fight, but in their commitment to listen, learn, and grow together.

Chapter 30: A New Dawn

As dawn broke over the valley, the light spilled across the land, illuminating the remnants of the gathering. The previous night had been a turning point, a delicate dance between tension and reconciliation that had reinforced the importance of their alliance.

Moshoeshoe rose early, his mind swirling with thoughts of the future. The events of the previous evening weighed heavily on him. While they had avoided disaster, the underlying issues that threatened their unity still loomed.

In the days following the gathering, Moshoeshoe called for another council meeting. He understood that they needed to solidify their bonds and ensure that misunderstandings were addressed before they could fester again.

Gathered in the council chamber, the leaders from both communities took their seats. Moshoeshoe looked around, sensing both apprehension and determination. *"We have faced challenges together and celebrated our unity,"* he began. *"But we must confront the shadows that linger. How do we move forward?"*

Mantsopa spoke first. *"We need a committee focused on fostering communication between our tribes. This can help address grievances before they escalate. We cannot afford to let misunderstandings divide us."*

Sizwe added, *"We should also establish regular joint events—cultural exchanges, workshops, and training. This will help us understand one another better and strengthen our ties."*

The council nodded in agreement, and they began to formulate a plan that would build on the goodwill fostered during the recent gathering. They established a framework for ongoing dialogue and collaboration, aiming to ensure that every voice was heard and valued.

As the weeks passed, the alliance flourished. The communities participated in joint projects—cultivating shared gardens, hosting storytelling nights, and engaging in friendly competitions. These events not only celebrated their cultures but also deepened their understanding of one another.

Moshoeshoe watched with pride as the barriers began to dissolve. Old rivalries transformed into friendships, and the laughter of children echoed through the valley, a testament to the healing power of unity.

However, as the alliance thrived, whispers of conflict still echoed from beyond their borders. The neighboring tribe remained wary, and rumors of war persisted. Moshoeshoe knew that they could not become complacent.

One evening, he gathered the council once more. *"We have made great strides, but we must not ignore the external threats,"* he cautioned. *"We need to continue strengthening our defenses while fostering peace."*

Sizwe and Mantsopa agreed, and they decided to hold a joint training exercise with both tribes' warriors. This would serve as a demonstration of their unity, showcasing their commitment to peace while remaining prepared for any potential conflict.

On the day of the exercise, warriors from both communities gathered, their faces determined. Moshoeshoe addressed them, his voice ringing with conviction. *"Today, we show not only our strength but our commitment to each other. We stand together, not as rivals, but as allies."*

The training was a blend of strategy, skill, and camaraderie, a testament to their shared goals. As the sun set over the valley, the warriors stood shoulder to shoulder, the atmosphere charged with unity.

But as they celebrated their achievements, a messenger arrived with urgent news: the neighboring tribe had mobilized, and a contingent was marching toward their borders.

The council met immediately, tension palpable. *"We cannot let them see us as weak,"* Sizwe urged. *"We must prepare for battle."*

Moshoeshoe felt the weight of leadership heavy upon him. *"But we must also consider diplomacy. We cannot let fear dictate our actions. Let's send an emissary to convey our commitment to peace."*

With a deep breath, he chose Sizwe to deliver the message, understanding that he was best suited to navigate the complexities of negotiation. *"Go forth and seek dialogue,"* he instructed. *"But be prepared for anything."*

As Sizwe set out, the community held its breath, anxiously awaiting the outcome. Days passed, each moment stretching into eternity. Tension simmered in the air as both sides prepared for the worst.

Finally, Sizwe returned, his expression grave. *"They are willing to talk, but only if we demonstrate our strength first,"* he reported. *"They wish to see that we are united and prepared."*

The council deliberated, knowing the stakes were high. They decided to hold a public display of their strength—a demonstration of their alliance that would communicate their readiness to defend their territory while reinforcing their commitment to peace.

On the appointed day, warriors from both tribes gathered, showcasing their skills and strategies in a show of unity. The atmosphere was charged, a powerful testament to their collective strength.

As the demonstration concluded, Moshoeshoe stepped forward, addressing the crowd. *"We stand here today, united against any threat. We will defend our lands, but we choose peace over war. Let our actions speak louder than words."*

A murmur of agreement swept through the crowd, and a sense of solidarity enveloped them. The neighboring tribe's leaders, observing from a distance, exchanged glances, their resolve wavering in the face of such unity.

In the days that followed, the neighboring tribe approached once more, this time with a willingness to negotiate. A council of elders from both tribes gathered to discuss their future, guided by Moshoeshoe's vision of peace.

As the discussions unfolded, they forged a new pact, one that recognized their shared interests and committed to mutual respect. The alliance was not just a shield against conflict; it became a beacon of hope for the surrounding tribes.

As the sun set over Thaba Bosiu, Moshoeshoe felt a sense of fulfillment wash over him. They had faced their fears, confronted the shadows of doubt, and emerged stronger.

In the months that followed, the landscape transformed, not just in physical form but in spirit. The communities flourished, built on trust and collaboration. Moshoeshoe and Mantsopa continued to lead, their vision for a united future becoming a reality.

As Moshoeshoe gazed out over the valley, he understood that the journey was ongoing. The road to unity was not without challenges, but with each step, they were weaving a tapestry of resilience that would endure.

Together, they would face whatever storms lay ahead, united in their commitment to peace, understanding, and the promise of a brighter future.

Epilogue: The Dawn of a New Era

Months passed since the establishment of the joint council, and the relentless drought continued to test the strength of the Basotho and Matabele alliance. Yet amid the trials, a sense of resilience had taken root within the hearts of the people. They worked together, sharing resources and supporting one another, transforming their desperation into determination.

As the sun rose over Thaba Bosiu one morning, casting a warm glow across the valley, Moshoeshoe stood on the mountaintop, contemplating the progress they had made. He felt a swell of pride as he watched children from both communities playing together, their laughter echoing through the air—a sound he had yearned for in the darkest of times.

Mantsopa approached him, her presence calming. *"We've come far, but the journey is far from over,"* she said, her eyes scanning the horizon. *"We must remain vigilant."*

"Indeed," Moshoeshoe replied. *"But I believe we've laid a strong foundation. The true strength of our alliance lies in our unity, and I see it blossoming every day."*

In the weeks that followed, they organized a festival to celebrate their resilience—a gathering that would solidify their bond and honor the struggles they had faced. Preparations were made, and excitement buzzed through the communities as they came together to plan a day of festivities.

On the day of the festival, the atmosphere was electric. Colorful banners adorned the gathering place, and the scent of traditional foods filled the air. Musicians played, and dancers showcased their heritage, weaving together the rich cultures of both peoples.

As Moshoeshoe addressed the crowd, he felt a profound sense of hope. *"Today, we celebrate our shared strength and resilience. We have faced challenges that could have torn us apart, yet here we stand—together. Let this festival be a reminder that our unity is our greatest weapon against adversity."*

Cheers erupted from the crowd, their spirits lifted as they embraced the moment. The joy of the festival overshadowed the struggles they had faced, if only for a while.

But as the celebrations continued, a shadow lurked at the edges of the gathering. Whispers of dissent still lingered among those who felt the alliance had not gone far enough. Moshoeshoe knew that their work was not finished. The path to true unity required ongoing effort and commitment.

As night fell and the stars twinkled above, Moshoeshoe and Mantsopa shared a quiet moment, watching the flickering fires and the laughter that filled the air. *"We've made it this far, but we must continue to listen and adapt,"* he said, his voice filled with resolve.

"True unity is a journey, not a destination," Mantsopa agreed. *"We must ensure that every voice is heard, especially those who feel marginalized."*

With renewed determination, they pledged to deepen their efforts, promising to keep the lines of communication open and address any grievances that arose. Their commitment to fostering understanding and solidarity became a guiding principle as they navigated the complexities of their alliance.

As the seasons changed and the rains finally arrived, the land began to heal, slowly but surely. Hope blossomed, not just in the fields but in the hearts of the people. The shared struggle had woven them together, creating a tapestry of resilience that would endure.

Years later, as Moshoeshoe looked back on the challenges they had overcome, he felt a profound sense of gratitude. The alliance between the Basotho and Matabele had not only survived but thrived, becoming a beacon of hope for neighboring communities facing similar struggles.

In his heart, he knew that the legacy of their journey would continue to inspire future generations. They had forged a path toward unity, transforming their suffering into strength, and proving that together, they could face any storm.

With Mantsopa by his side, he stood resolute, ready to lead his people into a future filled with promise and possibility, knowing that the power of unity would light their way.

Appendix

A. Historical Context

The Basotho people emerged in the early 19th century, primarily in what is now Lesotho. They faced pressures from both European colonizers and rival tribes. King Moshoeshoe I (1786–1870) played a crucial role in unifying various clans into a cohesive nation, navigating complex political landscapes marked by warfare and diplomacy.

B. Key Figures

1. *Moshoeshoe I*

Background: Born in the late 18th century, he became a skilled leader and strategist.

Achievements: Founded the Basotho nation, created a central government, and established strong diplomatic ties with neighboring tribes.

Legacy: Revered as a father figure of the Basotho, his strategies of alliance and negotiation laid the foundation for modern Lesotho.

2. *Mantsopa*

Background: A respected prophetess known for her wisdom and spiritual guidance.

Contributions: Provided counsel to Moshoeshoe, helping to shape his decisions and strategies during tumultuous times.

Significance: Represented the vital role of women in leadership and spirituality within Basotho culture.

C. Cultural Practices

Traditional Ceremonies: Include initiation rites, harvest festivals, and rainmaking rituals, reflecting the community's spiritual beliefs and connection to the land.

Warrior Culture: Emphasized bravery, loyalty, and skill in battle. Young men were trained from an early age, instilling values of honor and protection of the community.

Agricultural Practices: The Basotho primarily practiced subsistence farming, cultivating crops like maize and sorghum, and relied on livestock for both sustenance and status.

D. Language and Terminology

Sesotho: The language of the Basotho, rich in proverbs and oral traditions.

Key Terms:

"*Mokhosi*": A gathering or ceremony.

"*Thaba Bosiu*": The mountain that served as Moshoeshoe's stronghold, symbolizing strength and protection.

"*Lefika*": Traditional healers and spiritual leaders in the community.

E. Timeline of Events

1786: Birth of Moshoeshoe I.

1830s: Formation of the Basotho nation as clans unite.

1858: Establishment of the Basotho as a recognized political entity.

1868: Lesotho becomes a British protectorate, altering the dynamics of power.

F. Further Reading

"*Moshoeshoe: Founder of the Basotho Nation*" by D. M. W. Malefane: A comprehensive biography exploring the life and leadership of Moshoeshoe I.

"*A History of Lesotho*" by E. A. Smith: Provides an in-depth look at the historical developments in Lesotho and the impact of colonialism.

"*The Basotho: A History of the People*" by R. E. T. B. G. Morapeli: Explores the cultural practices and social structures of the Basotho.

G. Author's Note

Writing this novel was a journey of discovery into the rich history and culture of the Basotho people. It highlights the importance of understanding and preserving cultural narratives in a world that often overlooks their significance. I hope this story inspires readers to explore the themes of unity, resilience, and the power of collaboration in their own lives.

Acknowledgments

I would like to extend my heartfelt thanks to those who made this novel possible.

First, my deepest gratitude goes to my partner, Mosa Patricia Mpopo, for your unwavering support, encouragement, and belief in my vision. Your insights and enthusiasm have been invaluable throughout this journey.

I am also grateful to my family and friends for their patience and understanding as I immersed myself in this writing process. Your encouragement and feedback have helped shape this story into what it is today.

Special thanks to the historians and scholars whose works informed my understanding of the Basotho culture and the lives of Moshoeshoe I and Mantsopa. Your dedication to preserving history has inspired me deeply.

Finally, I extend my gratitude to the Basotho people, whose rich heritage and enduring spirit serve as the foundation of this story. I hope this novel honors your legacy and inspires others to learn about your incredible history.

Thank you all for being part of this journey.